# FINDING THE LOST LUMDIE

Linda McGeary

*Linda McGeary*

Cover Design
pgigraphics.com
Kenny and Mary Ann Pierce
2024

DEDICATION
to all people everywhere
who long for the
Peaceable Kingdom

# CHAPTER ONE

The rain subsides to a warm drizzle hovering in the air, more than falling, a muggy reminder of the coming rainy season. Across River Harapo the purple-blue of twilight tinges the southwestern sky. On the landing of the Hundred Steps of Heartsease, Zada Zan conceals herself behind a pillar, and watches a man in black metal armor approach her mother, Avril, the Mother Protector of Heartsease.

The man carries himself like a soldier, dresses like one, which is no surprise, as everyday there is an influx of fighting men arriving in the city of King Trabot NiVar. Soldiers are not frequenters of Heartsease. He is welcome but seems out of place here.

War is coming to Harapo City… Again.

The new invaders, the Daggale, want this fertile valley, just as the NiVar had wanted it three hundred years ago, when they pushed the peaceful Lumdie out into the Red Desert at the southwest end of our Aggadae Mountain Range.

We never knew who built Heartsease, or how long it had been here. It was here when we, the Aggadae, came. That was over a thousand years ago. We are a simple, plain people. We live on the mountain side in modest dwellings. We are the Keepers and Protectors, not in a warlike way, but live to keep the balance of life from the inner worlds to the outer.

When the Lumdie came to be our neighbors seven hundred years ago, they were good neighbors, peaceful, industrious. A happy people. We lived next to each other sharing the land. The Lumdie became the center of a trade route. Then the NiVar came and pitched their tents on the south side of the river, they sold their protection to the Lumdie against the occasional murderous marauders. They were paid well.

Zada hangs back, watching the exchange between her mother and the man. There is tension in her mother's shoulders, it is slight, no other would have noticed it, but Zada knows her mother well. The man shakes his clinched fist in Avril's face, but she stands resolute without flinching. Zada is too far away to hear more than the murmur of low voices. No distinct words. Zada leans forward straining to hear, her foot makes a small scraping noise against the pillar.

The man jerks his head toward the slight sound, listening with head cocked. He peers into the lengthening shadows towards where she hides, holding her breath, her body perfectly still. Not sure why she doesn't want him to see her, but the feeling of threat is palpable. He spins away suddenly, black cloak billowing behind him as he hurries down the Hundred Steps toward the Kings palace at the edge of Lake Harapo, and the city sprawling next to the river that exits the lake. Zada watches him go, with a release of breath. When she turns again to where her mother had been, Avril is gone.

Zada's thoughts turn to the coming war and to tales of the Lumdie. She grew up on stories of the peaceful neighbors, the Lumdie, industrious builders, and farmers, it had been a city of kind people, she was told. City Harapo was a marvel in stone. Running water, gardens, bathhouse's, a waste disposal system the envy of kings. Yet the Lumdie had no king and had been governed by the people. The Aggadae and Lumdie were friends. But not the NiVar.

The NiVar had lived in a tent city three hundred years ago, on the south side of the Harapo River. They were always a warlike people but kept the Lumdie safe from invaders, until one of their leaders, Trabot NiVar the First, decided he should have their riches, *all* their riches, not just what the generous Lumdie shared with the NiVar for keeping them safe, so Trabot NiVar the First, sacked Harapo City, made himself king and banished the Lumdie to the Red Desert never to be heard from again. But with them went the skill to keep the city functioning. According to Aggadae history it is only a pale shadow of its former glory. That first king built a crude palace, compared to Lumdie standards, at the choicest spot on Lake Harapo, where the present King, Trabot NiVar the Fifth, lived with his three queens, and many children.

But war is war, there is always someone who wants what someone else has, and is willing to kill or die for the chance to get it, and power over the people. They always think having more will make them happy. It never does... for long.

The NiVar left the Aggadae alone, believing they had no wealth to take, and were not being a threat, so they ignored them... mostly. The peaceful ways of the Aggadae and Lumdie didn't intrigue them.

Zada's people lived in the higher folds of the mountains overlooking Lake Harapo, River and City. They were Keepers of Heartsease for a thousand years. The holy place where people come for healing and respite when the world wearied them. Simple, hardworking people, judging few and helping many. Not all the Aggadae were Protectors with the white and purple hair, but they were all Keepers, peaceful... Like the Lumdie. She wondered what that meant for them in these uncertain times. How were they to survive savage people?

Zada knows where her mother is going and follows.

The heart of Heartsease is a large plain room filled with peace, a sacred place. On the dais is the glowing white stone altar at the north end of the room. Cushions are scattered on the polished black marble floor. Some people visiting for the first time think the floor is water and hesitate to venture forth. To see people sitting on the cushions is like seeing people on tiny boats floating on a calm black lake. She loves this room. The peace of the high altar blessing the people, the polished floor... and there is her mother... just where she thought she would find her, kneeling in front of the stairs leading up to the dais and altar.

No one speaks here. It is a silent room. A listening room.

As Zada approaches, Avril stands and turns. Avril takes Zada gently by the hand and leads her to their private chambers not far from the listening room. A large plain living space with a balcony overlooking the farmlands and city; and sleeping rooms for the family, which is only the two of them since her father, Avery, died two years ago, close to her sixteenth birthday. She misses him still, like a savage wound that won't heal. They were a close family. The three of them... and Jag, of course, her mother's Sand Cat, who is lazing on the balcony railing. He stretches, jumps to the floor and comes and sits at their feet, looking back and forth between them. He's family too, she thinks, grateful for him.

"What did that man want?" Alarm jangles Zada's nerves seeing the tear tracks on her mother's cheeks.

"What is it? Tell me!" Jag gives a rumble at Zada's harsh tone, and fluffs his fur making himself look bigger than his thirty pounds.

"It is time." Avril says.

# CHAPTER TWO

"Time for what, Mother?"

"For you to know the truth. The whole truth."

"The truth... what truth, about what?"

"The Lumdie and where they have gone. About you and what that man wants."

Zada's mother leads her to the most secluded room of their home and they sit on cushions against the stone wall, Jag rumbling between them.

"I know you know the Lumdie were lost to us. That much is somewhat true. But how and where they went, we have kept among the Protectors only. It's time for you to know the whole story."

"But, Mother..."

"No. Listen first. If you don't listen, you can't hear... Listen with no words in your mouth. No formulated thoughts in your mind. First, Listen!"

Zada nods, sinking into the silence as she's been taught to do since childhood.

"That man is one of King Trabot NiVar's allies, his name is Mollin, he believes there is treasure at Heartsease. I told him we have no treasure as they understand treasure, that Heartsease *is* the treasure. That its people *are* the treasure. He can't understand and doesn't believe me.

The King sent him to tell me if I don't give him the treasure of Heartsease to support his war, he will accept you as first payment. King Tarbot has heard of your unusual beauty. Mollin said he will come and take both by force if it is not given."

Zada is stunned out of *Listening*. Is she to be given to a cruel King to save her people? Jag puts his large paw on her knee as if to reassure her.

"No!" her mother says, "No!" as if she could read Zada's thoughts. "I would never allow that, but you and Jag must leave this place tonight and never return.

She blinks at Mother's words. Stung to the core, a cold flush infuses her body. Leave Heartsease? How could Mother expect her to do such a thing?

"You must find the lost Lumdie." Avril hands her the White Staff, to Zada's astonishment. Avril takes off the White Tabard and places it upon her daughter's shoulders.

"Mother…" Zada breathes through clinched teeth. She knows what this means. Her mother is passing the authority of Protection to her. "I…"

"No! It is time for the passing of the Staff and Tabard. These will protect you through the desert. The Staff will guide you, feed you, the Tabard will shelter you, and Jag will dream with you and guard you from harm."

"But…"

"You have always been told that the Lumdie were driven out… Only partly true. The Protectors saved as many as they could. In order to protect them, they sent them through the mountains on the Stone Path. Only the Protectors have known about the Path for centuries. Your Great, Great, Great Grandfather led the Lumdie with our other White Staff, and Tabard which was only for the Father Protectors to use. Took them to a place where they could not be found, enslaved or killed. We were unable to save them all, and some were sent out into the desert. But by doing this we divided our strength. You will find them and unite it again. Yes, the Lumdie did go out into Red Terra, not only to the west, but through the mountains, not to perish… but to survive. And now you too, *must go*."

"No, not without you!"

"You must. Mollin and the King will come back at the mark of midnight and you *must* be gone. We have to prepare for your journey."

"What is the Stone Path?"

"A way through the Aggadae Mountains. The way the Lumdie went to the other side and out onto the Red Desert. Those of us Keepers who have vowed to protect our sanctuary home for all people must stay and do our best. Even for those who may bring us death. We must hold true."

"I can't leave! I won't leave you!"

*"Yes! You will!"*

"Is this why you would never let me take my vows? Did you know this was coming?" Zada feels the pain of lose at having to leave her mother, her home. Tears prick her eyes as she looks up at her mother through the hedge of her wet lashes.

*"You are my treasure,* Daughter. I've taught you everything I can. Jag will dream you the rest."

"That makes no sense. You always said I was chosen from birth? But chosen for what, if not as the next Protector?"

"Oh, yes, dear child. From the moment you were born, you had the hair of a vowed Protector. We could all see you were special. Your white hair, two inches long, with deep purple roots at the crown, and brushed with lilac at the tips." Her mother's eyes softened, "For this time... You were chosen for this time. And even though your hair grows past your shoulders now, it has never changed its color. And that is how I know you are still chosen. Chosen for this time in our history. You."

Mother's words were firm, but spoken softly, with so much love in her eyes. Avril smiles and gently touches Zada's cheek. "I love you more than life itself. More than anything on Mother Terra." Avril stands, pulling Zada up with her, "Now it is time you go."

"Mother..." The tremble in Zada's voice breaks the dam of her tears and they fall like rain. "I don't want..."

"*I know.* This is hard." Avril holds Zada in a close embrace, and the two, cling together, for a long moment. They both take deep breaths and a long look into the loved face of the other, not knowing if they will ever see each other again.

"I know from the dreaming it will take you at least a week, maybe longer, to get through the mountain. You will not be alone. Jag will dream with you." Avril leads her out of the room.

In the common kitchens her mother prepares a travel pack, "This should last you at least through the mountains, maybe longer. Food and water enough for both of you. After that... The White Staff will feed you while you're in the desert of Red Terra. The Tabard will shelter you."

From the kitchens Mother takes Zada to the Listening Room up onto the dais, and to the back side of the white altar, where she presses one of the carved stone leaves on the back of the altar, a doorway scraps open within the large square altar stone. There are stairs leading down, down into the heart of the Aggadae Mountain Range.

"Mother… Please come with me."

"No, Daughter, this is where our path parts. Go, wrapped in the warmth and protection of my love. I will always be with you."

Avril bends down to nuzzle face to face with Jag, her cat. "Take good care of our Zada, teach her what comes next. You have been the best Sand Cat to ever live. Thank you!" She stands and Jag goes down the stairs, looking back from the bottom for Zada to follow.

Mother and daughter embrace each other one last time, then Zada turns, with uncertain courage, and follows Jag.

## CHAPTER THREE

Avril waits for the midnight hour. Heartsease sanctuary is alight with a thousand candles. The floor glows like water in moonlight. She will let them see the true treasure of this place. If they can… *see*… what is before them. This, she thinks, will impress King Trabot. He will *see* the sanctuary *is* the treasure. Or at least *see* its simple, elegant, beauty. He and his men will come soon.

Avril knows by reputation the king is a cruel man. She does not know if this night she will live or die. What she does know is that these men will not find her daughter. They might kill her and all of Aggadae, make a ruin of Heartsease looking for treasure… she shudders at this thought… a place her people have kept for a thousand years, and the NiVar would be the poorer for its ruin, but they would not have Zada Zan. The last Keeper-Protector of the White Staff and Cloak. The Tabard of One.

Closing her eyes, Avril prays aloud for the first time in this room of silent presence.

"Thank you, Spanner of Heaven, Founder of full moon's light and day sun's heat for growing things, for stars to light the night and for water like love's pure kiss. Protect… I pray. Thank You."

Avril breaths deeply and straightens her shoulders at the sound of a dozen marching men with metal spears, tap, tap, tapping the floor as they come. An act meant to intimidate she is sure. Avril hopes they don't chip the surface of the polished stone. Swords made small clanging noises upon their belts as they enter the candle-lit bedazzling room where Avril stands in front of the white altar with arms outstretched in welcome.

King Trabot NiVar stops, looking down at the floor, then hitches up his robes as if to keep them dry. He strides out onto shiny black stone. Some of his men began to do likewise until they see the Kings mistake and two of his youngest men begin to laugh. But not for long.

Blood splashes the pillars and floors of the sanctuary entrance. Mollin nearly slices their heads off in one blow of his long sword. Avril lets out a chocked scream, covering her mouth with both hands. A sad sacrilege against life, and against this holy place.

This was not a promising beginning. Avril hurries to greet the King, bowing low, thinking maybe a less formal setting might be better for this meeting.

"Please, come this way... I will have refreshments brough to the gathering room. The night is chilly, we have a fire set, we can light it for your comfort. Please follow me." Avril shudders then pulls herself into focus. She can't wait to get away from the metallic smell of blood.

Avril leads them to a room almost as large as the sanctuary. A place of fountains and pools where they can sit by the fireplace and talk. Away from the two dead men laying on the black marble floor of Heartsease. Her heart breaking at the unnecessary deaths of two such young but foolish men. The promise of their lives snuffed out too soon.

Avril knew from the stories told, the King is a vain and proud man, as well as cruel. Not one to be laughed at... so, when he walked right out onto the reflecting pool and sank to his thighs with a shocked scream of rage, she knew she had made a huge mistake, a second mistake, that would look calculated on her part.

No one laughed this time.

She held her breath as he climbed out of the pool and stomped up to her dripping wet, short sword drawn. She held perfectly still. Her eyes wide, expecting to die on the spot.

King Trabot NiVar balled his fist and struck her... hard, knocking her to the floor, giving her a vicious kick in the stomach, doubling her in half.

"Where is your daughter?" He yells, "and the treasure I came for. Don't think to make a fool of me, woman."

"There is no gold, or silver, or precious gems. There never has been." Avril said gasping in pain on the floor. "The only treasure *is* Heartsease itself. It is what the people of Aggadae value." Avril doesn't dare to look up from the floor. "We have no wealth. We are not that kind of temple." She coughs, gasping again for breath. "What little we have as families you may take." Deep breath, "What wealth we had in times past was taken long ago by your ancestors. I swear it."

"Not according to Mollin, he says all temples have gold. Tell me where it is, and where your daughter is! Or I will have to question every white and purple hair oddity in this place. You will tell me! I will find out. You will give what treasures you have or I will tear this place down to its foundations. I will burn the hills and your sacred garden groves. I will set this mountain on fire. Now, where is this beauty, Zada Zan, Mollin tells me he has seen in the streets of Harapo?"

"I don't know. She fled out into the Red Desert when I told her you were coming for her."

*"You lie!"* He turned to his men, "Take this retched creature to my palace and put her in shackles, chain her to the wall in the deepest darkest hole to be found. Tear - this - place - apart." He screams, fire in his eyes, his feet wet, standing in a puddle. "Kill anyone who refuses to give you the treasure I seek... and find that damn girl."

Avril's heart sings with silent joy even as did the stones of Heartsease, glad Zada is out of his reach.

As hard as it was, she had done the right thing sending Zada away. The King's men pull Avril from the floor, chain her wrists and ankles and lead her out of Heartsease for the last time. The sound of ruin dogging her shuffling steps.

# CHAPTER FOUR

At the bottom of the stairs, Jag waits. Zada knocks the staff on the bottom step, just as her mother told her to do, and the step cracks in half, and a green sprig of a growing thing springs up, a cling vine, she thinks, and it begins to ascend the stairs with the sound of breaking stone, green filling the stairway.

Jag turns, *heruffing* her to come along.

Zada has never known a time when her mother didn't have Jag as a companion. She worries how she will manage Heartsease without him. Will there *be* a Heartsease after tonight?

The Stone Path, a tunnel maybe ten people wide at the beginning, but too deep and dim to see very far as it stretches away from Zada. Then she notices the White Staff is glowing at the top, a foot above her head, a soft yellow light, like a torch.

"I didn't know it could do that," she whispers.

People thought the White Staff of oak wood and the White Tabard of leather were only objects of leadership, signs of the Mother Protector. But all the Keepers knew better. The Tabard could give you warmth when you were cold or cool you when you were hot. The Staff could grow things. Bring water and healing to the land, and its people. She hadn't known it could bring light as well.

If only King Trabot had known about the Staff and Tabard, he'd have come for them. But maybe they don't work for anyone not chosen, committed and faithful, who believed, or is in need of what it can provide.

Jag keeps walking, leading her. Close to a bend in the tunnel, he stops and looks back. Zada picks up the heavy pack, shouldering it onto her back. They walk until the light of the staff dims hours later. Jag curls on the stone floor and covers his face with his tail. Zada sits the pack down, exhausted, and curls next to the Sand Cat to sleep.

*****

When Zada wakes hours later, Jag is staring at her. She rouses herself and sits up. The tail of a dream clouding her mind. She yawns, and scratches him under his chin, and his head around the ears. She grew up with this animal, she knows what he likes. Jag is a beautiful wheat sand color with black tipped ears, muzzle, tail tip and paws. She loves Jag almost as much as she loves her mother. Since the death of her father, Zada has come to see Jag and her mother almost as one thing. Thinking of her mother now pulls on a thread of the dream she'd had, and in her mind, she sees the coming of King Trabot and his men. The scene of him pulling up his robes and the two who laughed... and died. Then his watery humiliation. Her mother standing stone still. It was a dream... wasn't it? Then she knew what her mother meant, 'Jag will dream with you.' She is astonished, "You see things... don't you?" She says, Jag stares back as if in agreement.

She leaps to her feet grabbing the pack. "He will kill her, Jag. He will kill her for witnessing such a humiliation." Zada turns back toward home. Jag leaps in front of her, bristling, a deep throaty growl halting her. She has never seen him like this before. She sits down in front of him.

"What am I supposed to do? I can't let them kill her. *You* can't let them kill her." A painful knot settles in her chest.

"There's no way back up those stairs... is there, Jag?"

Jag comes to Zada with a head butt and a rumbling purr. Forehead to forehead. She closes her eyes, and swallows the lump in her throat, arms around the comforting presence of the Sand Cat.

"Yes... I know... There is nothing to be done but go forward. Find the Lumdie. No matter what I want. It is the thing to do. The right thing. It is what she wants. I was born for this. Born with the purple and white hair of the Vowed Heartsease Protectors. "But... if it is all lost, what does it mean for me now, Jag, to be a Protector of Heartsease? Even the Mother Protector?"

*****

The tunnel is sometimes narrow, only wide enough for one person to go through at a time. Other places it is wide like a cave with a low ceiling, a small crowd of ten to thirty people might fit in these places, but the outer limits are too dark to see, even with the Staff's light. But the sounds echo like a large open space. Empty. Zada feels the Staff pull in the way they should go, ever so slightly when they have to cross one of these large open dark spaces. She can only see a few yards at a time.

There are cracks and fissures along the walls in places, and once, there was one split in the ceiling of the tunnel that went straight up like a chimney and let in some light and rain. When they settle down for the night -- anyway she thinks it is night -- Zada hears the slither of living things, sometimes making it hard to sleep, when the staff dims. There's really no way to tell if it's night when you don't have a hint of light other than the White Staff. Zada calculates they have been walking for three days, if you count the sleep times as night. So, she hopes maybe halfway to the desert. She can't wait to see the sky overhead. She would forgo sleep to get out of this place faster. It is cold, dank, and smells like... she doesn't know what it smells like... just old and closed in... she shivers... like a snake's den.

Later that day the Staff dims its light, a sign she's learned means stop and rest, eat, sleep. Zada takes off the pack and sits with her back against the rock wall. Jag flops down beside her, waiting for food to emerge from the pack when they hear the slither and clack of toenails on stone. Not a small animal sound. Zada had seen a small lizard in the tunnel, Jag caught and ate it. This was not that sound. She grabs the staff from the floor and leaps to her feet, as does Jag, instantly alert. Zada knocks the staff against the floor and illumination spans the tunnel from side to side and a long way down the Stone Path.

The lizard is twice again the thirty-pound weight of Jag, and three times as long, its tail whipping about. The creature is supple and hungry looking. Jag wasn't going to eat *this* lizard, and she had no weapon to protect them. Jag put himself between Zada and the monster. It moves fast like a river croc. Maybe they're related she thinks, it fakes a lunge, then backs off, intent on luring Jag closer.

She crowds it on the open side, distracting it just long enough for Jag to leap on its back and sink tooth and claw deep into the head and neck. It writhes, screaming, then runs against the wall trying to dislodge the cat. Both are screeching an ungodly racket, the echo bouncing down the tunnel. Jag bites harder, ripping, clamping on an ear hole, tearing at it fiercely. Blood runs down the lizard's face, it flings droplets about trying to rid itself of the cat clinging to its head and long neck. Then it whips Jag with its tail, knocking him off. Jag flips, falling and the savage creature grabs one of Jags front paws in its mouth and shakes its head, jerking, as Jag claws at it with his other three paws and howls in pain.

Zada hits the lizard a good solid whack with the staff to the side of its head near the damaged ear hole. It drops Jag, and comes after her. She thumps the staff on the stone floor like she had seen her mother do a thousand times when growing things. Cling vines whipped up from cracks in the stone and binds the lizard to the wall. The vines grow tighter and thicker all the way to the top of the tunnel. It struggles but can't free itself. It screams and thrashes in rage at its lost meal, but there is no escape.

Zada hopes it doesn't have a family somewhere nearby to hear its angry distress.

Bending to inspect Jags foot she touches the Staff to the bloody mangle and it begins to heal. Relief fills her. She washes it clean, gives him a drink and herself, then she grabs their pack and strides away.

"Come on Jag. Not a friendly place to nap."

Limping, Jag follows.

After that they don't sleep much and it takes them four, maybe five days in total, to exit Stone Path; a small hole in the side of the mountain leading out onto Red Terra. A hot, dry, dusty place of cracked, barren red earth with nothing on the horizon but wind.

Zada remembers what her mother told her. "Knock the staff on the opening and move away quickly from the mountain."

She strikes the mouth of the cave they had just come out of. The mountain's voice rumbles and the hole begins to fill up with broken stones. The mountain shakes. Zada stumbles backwards, covering her head with her arms and the White Staff. They run out into the desert to escape the tunnels collapse and rock-slide down the side of the mountain.

Truly, immutably, now there is no way home.

# CHAPTER FIVE

Zada collapses to the ground, unable to go another step. She and Jag have been traveling for two days out on the cracked, flat, red desert. They are out of water, and food. She doesn't know how Jag can stand his fur in this heat, even though he is a Sand Cat, and she knows they originally came from the desert, that must mean something good for him, at least most of him was a light wheat sand color which absorbs less of the suns heat than the darker color. Such a dry heat, she has never experienced.

Waves of heat rise up from the ground like dry rain going the wrong direction.

She has the Tabard. It cools her in the hottest part of the day. And keeps them warm at night when the desert temperatures drop so drastically. It changes shape and covers them like a small tent or blanket when they sleep. She can stay cool in the day but she worries constantly about Jag over-heating with the exertion of walking. At least his foot is completely healed. Amazing as it is, even when she knows, has seen healing before, but, when it works by her hand, she is awed and humbled, to have that kind of power move through her to another. And so grateful.

Without Jag to dream with her she would be without solace.

Now, she relieves herself of the pack, empty but never the less, it felt like a weight she can't bear to carry another step. She lays down putting her head on it and Jag comes to snuggle against her. She pulls the Tabard over them both. A nap from the heat of the day will be good. She can figure out the food thing when they wake. They are asleep almost immediately.

*The night sky stars blink on one by one and the blue-black fills with points of light. She and Jag travel north by the light of those stars. At dawn Zada strikes the Staff to the red earth and water springs forth. Water and a fruit tree, a nut tree and some small harmless lizards come for the water. It takes the trees all day to grow and produce food, they rest in the shade. Jag hunts lizards.*

Zada stretches, yawns, and sits up, dawn light reforming the Tabard, more like the sleeveless cloak with a hood as it had been before. The dream shimmering like a mirage in her mind, even as the heat of the desert begins to climb. But she stands up and thumps the Staff to the ground. A wet spot appears. Then a bubble of water, then a gush. The sweet sound of leaping water. She thumps twice more and two tiny green and brown sprigs of new birth breaks through the wet ground.

"Ah ha!" she laughs, Jag laps at the spring thirstily. Zada pulls out the empty water flasks and fills them all. Then drinks what she needs, and sits back and watches the trees grow.

"I think I'm getting the hang of this dreaming thing, Jag. Without you, I would truly be more lost than the Lumdie."

They rest, sleep, eat; gather nuts, apples and lizards, then sleep some more. At nightfall they head north by starlight. They travel this way for five nights before they have to bring up another spring and trees. This time there are two kinds of fruit, and a type of root, and a different kind of nut. More lizards come. Jags favorite.

Zada wonders how she can tell which way is north every night when she can't see the direction of the sun. But somehow, their movement always feels right. Maybe her Staff really does know the way. Maybe it is following the first White Staff to cross this desert as if there is an invisible line connecting them, Great, Great, Great Grandfather who led the Lumdie across this desert. Mother said the Staff would guide her. She also has dreams of her mother, locked in a dungeon, but alive. Without much light, but someone brings her food and water. This is a great relief from her fearful imaginings.

*From the cracks of the red baked earth a swarm of giant hairy black and red scorpions flow, tails curl over their backs, like an army marching straight toward them. The sun high and hot. The scorpions are the size of a large man's hand. These were called by the people of the valley, the King of Scorpions. One sting is poison enough to kill a grown man. And this swarm was in the hundreds.*

Zada and Jag are wide awake at the same instant and on their feet. The Tabard shrinking to the long cloak upon waking. Their eyes taking some time to adjust to the brightness of daylight. They stand guarding each other's backs looking in every direction.

"There they are, Jag. Look at the size of those things. As big as a man's fist, hairy, black and red, that stinger must be an inch long. King Scorpions. Did we wake up from the dream to soon? I didn't see what we're supposed to do to keep ourselves safe with that many coming against us at once?"

She uses the only protection she has. The Staff. She strikes the earth a might blow and one of the cracks in the red desert fills up with water. She blinks in the glare of sunlight and heat. she doesn't think her heart has ever beat so hard. She had seen a man die of a King Scorpion sting once, it wasn't pretty. And it wasn't fast.

The water in the crack forces the crack wider, creating a brook stretching away in both directions between them and the scorpions on the other side. Do scorpions like water? Can they swim? A fact she can't recall. Maybe they don't like water.

Just as she thinks this, one jumps in the brook and makes its way across. She smashes it with the Staff as it climbs out of the water. And something begins to grow. Then, another crosses, and another. Each one she smashes begins to grow a tough rusty red wood-like plant. All along the bank of the brook the scorpions come. Jag slapping them back into the water when they get too close to her. The brook all the while expanding, making itself wider, longer. As the fertilized scorpion plants grow, Zada realizes it is a thorny hedge curling partway around them and also following the straight line of the brook. A wall of thorns, twisting and weaving together with spikes as long as her arm.

Looking across the widening brook she sees thousands of scorpions coming up out of the cracks beyond the brook. The ground shakes with them, she can barely breathe. Then she realizes it isn't the scorpions that are shaking the ground... it is a herd of wild desert boar. A stampede of them in a cloud of dust. And the hedge of scorpion thorns is now as tall as her, and it hides them, protects them. A shield for her and Jag against the boars. The relief she feels behind their hedge is beyond measure. She takes a deep breath, and almost laughs out loud, but doesn't, not wanting to alert the herd of their presences behind the thorns.

A blessing hidden among a misfortune, that is one of Mothers favorite sayings. The two often come wrapped together. And you never know which will come out of the box first.

She has heard wild pigs love to eat scorpions. She hasn't believed it.

But now she has to… because they are eating them by the hundreds. Gobbling them noisily, crunching, and snorting. A smell that is bitter bright rises from their gory mouths. The boar herd eats them like they are delicacies throwing back their heads and bellowing.

A sound Zada hopes to never hear again in her life. She shivers, remembering someone saying wild boar will eat people or almost anything that moves if they are hungry enough. She hadn't believed that either… a thing she no longer doubted.

Grateful for the hedge between, she thanks the scorpions for their sacrifice, just as she had for the lizards that fed Jag.

Zada and Jag wait quietly behind the hedge until the herd finishes eating and wallowing in the muddy brook cooling themselves and finally, sated on scorpions, they wander away not bothering to try the defense of the thorn hedge or find a way around it. Once the heard of wild boar are out of sight, she breaths easier. She and Jag, using the last of the daylight move north, thankful the herd went south.

# CHAPTER SIX

They travel for a week of nights with no further incidences until they come to a different kind of desert. White sand dunes. Hard on the eyes in daylight. Hard on legs walking up and down the hills of shifting sand which drains their energy, and supplies. The grains of sharp-edged sand, getting into everything when the wind blows, which is almost constant. This is far worse than the hard-baked, cracked Red Desert. And nothing grows here, and no water comes when the Staff calls it.

How could the Lumdie have come this way? How could ten thousand people, men, women and children, have survived such a place? This landscape strips away hope and courage. These dunes seem to go on forever. Certainly, there is no way people from Harapo could track her and Jag out here even if they are looking for her in this direction... which is unlikely. She knows her mother told them that she had followed the river west to that part of Red Terra.

It is a good thing they called a spring forth, fruit trees and filled up their flasks and pack at the edge of the dunes before crossing them. Six nights of up one dune, and sliding down the other side till they finally come to more solid ground again. Still sandy and white, but smaller more manageable dunes now.

A mountain range stretches out on the horizon. Something different to look at. They are getting close. Zada can feel it, courage revives. There is some plant life showing here and there, an occasional scrub oak or bitter brush. A hopeful sign. The Staff can produce water and fruit trees again.

"All is well." She smiles thinking of Mothers other favorite saying. "And it came to pass... Thankfully it didn't come to stay. All things change."

Still, the monotony of seeing the rise and fall of small dunes, even if they are more manageable, leaves Zada wondering, calculating their days traveled; four or five in the Stone Path. Seven or eight nights on Red Terra, now six nights on the shifting White Dunes... that was... seventeen or maybe twenty... or more if you count the rest days.

"Oh, I don't know." Zada says shaking her head, talking to herself as much as to Jag. "But I bet this will take another five to seven days of travel at least... it's hard to tell how far those mountains are from us." Sometimes she talks out loud just to break the windblown silence, even if Jag seldom voices a meow in reply. She would talk for as long as it took for her mouth to become dry and she had to drink some water. Fatigue dogged them.

Jag stops dead in his tracks, and fluffs himself, neck stretched out sniffing the air, scanning the sand. Zada knows what that means. *Danger*. She hopes it isn't more scorpions. She holds perfectly still as well, all fatigue frightened out of her, looking in an arc, around Jag and herself. There is movement beneath the white sand. An S shape, moving slowly towards them. On the other side of Jag, another.

She raises the Staff ready to strike any threat. That S shape under the sand can only mean one thing.

Sand vipers.

Her courage sinks. The one thing she fears more even than scorpions are sand vipers.

A gold wedge-shaped head pops out of the sand, tongue flicking the air. She whacks the head as hard as she can and the viper's full, five or six, foot length, twists away in the air, flying high. When it lands it looks dead, but it's hard to take her eyes off the limp thing. Jag moves like an arrow towards something just behind her right shoulder. When she turns, a sand viper is raised to a striking pose three feet of its body erect, weaving. Jag clamps it in his jaws shaking it fiercely, nearly biting its head off. The sand seems alive with S shaped movements. Jag drops the dead thing.

"Run, Jag," she shouts, "Run."

They run until dark fall. They finally stop to drink. She illuminates the Staff all around them. The sands are still. The moon is almost full. They rest for a short time, eat and drink, then continue to walk toward the mountain range. She feels so skittish there's no way for her to settle down for a sleep. Jag seems back to his normal self, no longer showing any sign of danger. So, when exhaustion finally pulls Zada to the ground to sit beside him, it is all she can do to pull the Tabard over them as the sun comes up.

"Are we safe?" she whispers, yawning, eyes closing. "That was terrifying. I never want to see another sand viper for the rest of my life… or scorpions… or boars… in fact I don't much like adventuring out here on the desert. Maybe we should go back to traveling by day." Another huge yawn escapes her. "At least it doesn't seem as hot here as it did days ago on the dunes." She pulls the Tabard snugly around Jag and holds him close. "Thank you for saving my life." He purrs, his head next to her ear, content, at peace, they sleep.

After they wake, they walk most of the day as it lengthens into night. In the morning, when the sun is straight up, they stop. Calling for a spring with the Staff. And trees for shade and food. The ground is still a lighter honey color instead of the Red Terra color, but it's about the same kind of dry-cracked earth. It feels solid and reassuring.

They resume their night time walking as the moon is high and lights their way for the next few days.

As they draw nearer to the mountain range, she sees it is very different from the mountains she is used to. These are red, pink, and sometimes purple or bluish. A horizontal strip running along the cliff front. Tall, much taller and straight up than she thought seeing them from a distance. It seems like they just keep going west and east. They are very unusual, flat-topped rock formations, where the mountains she has lived on were peaked and rimmed with pine trees. Trees will only grow where dirt can collect. These mountains or cliffs are mostly solid rock. They look like vertical hard sand. Sandstone? She has heard of sandstone before.

Here there are many more kinds of bitter brush out on the desert. More scrub oak, and juniper up against the cliffs. Some so sheer and tall they dazzle Zada with their beauty and difference. But where are the Lumdie? How could anyone climb these mountains straight up?

She and Jag camp up next to bushes that grow up against the red rock, a long narrow width of bushes that swerves like a curtain as far as the eye can see.

Zada calls for a fountain and fruit trees of several kinds and some root plants.

Exhaustion takes them through a full night's sleep, the first on the desert since shortly after they started out.

CHAPTER SEVEN

*The sun streams down through the leaves of apple, peach and fig trees. Dappling the shade, cooling the pinkish sand. Close to the trees, a tuft of sawgrass is growing up through the pink sand. The spring splashes musically over variegated stones and moves along making a brook following the Sandstone Mountains towards the west. The red, pink and blue colors of the horizontal strips are comforting. They sing like the silent room at Heartsease when things are at peace.*

*Jag is sitting still as the mountain, but not a danger sort of still. An almost eager, excited still. Then Zada sees the other Sand Cat sitting on a jutting rock in the scrub. Then another, larger, darker cat, bigger even than Jag. And a path into the bushes. A dark mouth of a small cave entrance, where another perfectly white Sand Cat sits in the shade. A beautiful smaller female Sand Cat and Jag are staring intently at each other.*

Zada wakes slowly to the babble of brook and birdsong. There seems to be dozens of red and blue birds in the trees, feasting on the ripe fruit. She looks for Jag, where she last saw him in their dream. The other Sand Cats are there. And the white one. Seeing her in full sunlight Zada realizes her ears are tinged lilac along with muzzle and tail-tip and paws. How strange. Then she sees the darker purple marking her forehead.

Jag moves toward her. They butt heads as if they are old friends. Then the other two come and they all greet each other even as more Sand Cats show up. The joy Zada feels coming from them is overwhelming. It brings tears of happiness to her eyes, as if this is a reunion of family, and she can't even say why she feels so moved by their greetings.

The crowd of jubilant Sand Cats lounge in the shade and eat Jags dried lizard supply, as if they know where to get live ones, so not to worry. She sits off by herself, enjoying the meowing, purring communication, the nuzzling among them. A very social gathering. She is enveloped with the same, Spirit feeling, she often had while sitting in front of the White Altar at Heartsease. She ponders this. And the Sand Cats.

She always thought cats were solitary creatures. So many of her assumptions were shifting. She feels her foundations shaken. Her entire life is not at all what she thought it would be a year ago, when the talk of war rose on the horizon and put fear in the hearts of her people. Many more people had been coming to Heartsease of late and Mother always spent time with them. Then took them to the Listening Room. This space, with the Sand Cats and the birds feels every bit as sacred as Heartsease.

Maybe the lesson here is that Heartsease is carried inside one's self. That there is an altar space within each person that travels with them.

Zada wonders about the meaning of life.

The questions? And answers! The discoveries.

How do you find truth in living experience, moral value in relationships, joy from humble acceptance of what is enough?

Did the Sand Cats all live in that small cave? How did they know another Sand Cat is in their territory? And why is the white one marked as she is? None of the other cats have a hint of lilac or purple in their fur.

She hopes their next dreaming would be more useful to finding the Lumdie. Were they on the other side of these Sandstone Mountains? Is she to go to the right or the left? How was Jag to know that? But he did manage to see things, like the dream of Mother in a prison cell. A horrible dungeon, and even though she was still alive it made Zada feel heavy inside, like her heart weighted a ton.

That night they all bed down together. Zada is quite warm with a pile of Sand Cats clustered about her. She falls asleep with a smile on her face.

*****

*Avril drinks gratefully the cup of cold water. "Thank you, young man."*
*She hands the cup back through the bars. "And thank you for taking off*

the chains from my ankles and wrists. I can't tell you what a blessing you are."

The young man grunts but says nothing to her. He goes back to his post, sits on the three-legged stool and throws dice against the wall. He has an older brother which Avril doesn't like at all. He is a mean one. Always has the watch shift after this one. No, she doesn't like him, but she loves him, has compassion for him. Feels sorry for the choses he's made. But she knows he has a closed heart, hard as stone. But this one…

"My name is Avril," she says. "What's your name?"

The young man glances at her, she can tell he is angry… oh, not at her. Maybe the older brother, though. She had watched them on several occasions throwing dice. The younger one here, maybe fifteen, discovered the brother's dice were weighted.

"So that's how you always win. You cheat!" he had said the last time they played.

"Just trying to teach my little brother how the world works." That one had sneered, scooping up the coins and pocketing them. "Father told me to toughen you up. You'll never last the war when it comes if you don't understand that. In this world, it's kill or be killed." That was the last night.

"Baz," He answers her softly, still throwing the dice against the wall with a clatter.

"The cheater is Uddo. Father's favorite, the eldest son. Uddo hates me because my mother, Father's third wife, is his favorite. But then Uddo hates all our siblings and father's other women. Did you know my father is King Trabot NiVar the Fifth? He has a lot of favorites. And many enemies."

Baz turns to face Avril then. "You're his favorite prisoner. He loves to hate you. You humiliated him. And he is planning a particularly ugly death for you on my mother's birthday tomorrow. He talks about it endlessly, to anyone who will listen. And they all listen… He is the king after all. He could put them all in dungeons like this if the whim struck him. He seems to hate everyone. Even his favorites sometimes." Baz frowned, "It's like a sickness…"

"Hate is a fire, Baz, it burns everything to ash." Avril sees his naked soul. Hurt, alone, hungry to be loved. She knows a soul unloved, or thought to be unloved, is capable of many evils.

*"Don't go down that path."* Avril sends him a wave of empathy. She may not have the White Staff, but she still has her human heart. *"Even if the NiVarian King rips my heart from my chest. It will never satisfy him."*

Baz takes a deep breath, *"I know that,"* and sighs.

Avril lets the silence build.

*"I have many brothers and sisters none of which I'm close to. I feel more acceptance from you than any one of them. To them, I'm just odd."*

Baz comes and unlocks the door. *"I've been thinking about doing this for a long time. It's not right a gentle soul like you to be in a place like this. It wasn't right that Father destroyed your temple and killed your people. I will help you. Will you help me escape from them?"*

*****

Zada rouses herself and looks over at the still sleeping Jag, curled beside him is the white female.

That was the strangest dream yet. It is like she was inside her mother's mind, seeing from her mother's eyes, and hearing from her ears. But then she thought, why not? Jag had dreamt with Mother for decades.

The excitement that her mother might be freed is thrilling. The other side of that news, is that Heartsease and the Aggadae people are no more. This brings unbearable pain. She wants to look away. Not see it, not feel it, not know it, but there it is. And she can't look away. That would be wrong. It would be to deny the truth. And she couldn't see how that comes out well.

Grief wets her face and she mourns the loss of her people, her place. She slips back into a slow and troubled sleep, comforted by the many Sand Cats curled against her.

# CHAPTER EIGHT

*Zada sees a man. Skin as black as midnight, white hair with purple at the crown, and fading lilac at the tips. He is waiting for them in a sandstone passageway. The white female Sand Cat runs to him bounding off a low rock wall and leaps onto his broad shoulders and perches there like it's her place by right of love.*

*"Welcome home, Zada. I'm Sinacrib" His smile is wide and sweet. He pats the Sand Cat sitting on his shoulders, "This is Ollish. We've been waiting for you." The crowd of cats surrounds him. Even Jag is there at his feet. A shaft of dazzling sunlight illuminates them all, surrounded by the colorful swervey sandstone walls.*

*****

She wakes with a start. All the cats come awake at the same moment, as if they were all in the same dream together with her. Maybe all Sand Cats can dream with people. She only had Jag to compare them to. And she had not known he could dream with Mother or herself until recently.

Today. Today will be the end of her journey. Or maybe the beginning. She had not known the Lumdie were a dark-skinned people. Mother had never mentioned it. To Mother it was most likely irrelevant. To her, people were simply people, with interesting differences.

Jag is urging her up. All the cats are shaking with excitement.

One after the other they go into the small cave opening. Zada follows them, squeezing into the small space, pushing her full pack in front of herself with one hand while pulling the Staff along with the other. This is the smallest cave yet as far as tunnels are concerned. She'd hoped to never see another one, but she crawls after Jag and the others. She trusts the dream… and the cats. After some time on her knees, she comes out into a tall vertical crack in the sandstone, it goes all the way up into blue. A passageway that twists off into open sky hundreds of feet above her. Jag is waiting for her to stand up. She puts on the pack and follows the Sand Cats.

The shapes and colors, the slant of light striking the stone is breathtakingly beautiful. At a pool of water in a rounded basin they all drink. It is the best water she has ever tasted. When she looks up from her cupped hands, there is Sinacrib, smiling. A tall, broad man with kind eyes. They shake hands and he hugs her.

"Welcome home, little sister." He turns and leads them to where the passage splits into three ways. "The other two are false leads Mother Terra has placed in the stone, to confuse any unwelcome enemies. And if you didn't know this one isn't… you'd come to believe it is too. But we know the way through." He indicates Ollish and the other cats. "They were so excited to meet your Sand Cat. They have dreamed with him many times and were eager to welcome him home. They all know each other very well."

*Life is a mystery*, she thinks. *Learning, always learning new thing on top of new things.*

They walk for the rest of the morning until the sun is hanging directly above them.

"Time for a break. I smell fruit in your pack and water."

The two of them settle on a stone ledge about the height of a bench, to eat, and rest, with the cats all napping on the sandy path. With the sun moving west, the passage's east side has light glancing off the curl of the walls.

"This is beautiful stone." Zada smooths her hand over the ledge they are sitting on. "I've never seen any stone like it in all of Harapo."

"We are hundreds of miles from there. The geography is very different here."

"The stone is so colorful."

"Our homes are carved into the heart of this stone. It's hard work, but it gives beautiful results. We have made a place for you and Jag while we waited for you to come across the desert. I think you will like it. It's right next to the marketplace stalls and work places. Close to the lake and the Grandfather Tree. And the center. You will have so many people wanting to show you our city. Your new home."

The Sand Cats begin to stir.

"Looks like they think it's time to leave." Sinacrib pulls Zada to her feet and picks up her pack.

"You don't have to do that." Zada smiles when he shoulders it up on his own broad back. "I think you've been carrying this long enough."

"Thank you," she says with a sigh of relief and another smile.

Within the hour they are at a place in the passage that is a swirling knot of blue, pink and purple stone what appears to be a dead end. But the Sand Cats scramble up into what looks like a bowl and the back side of another rounded shape and corner, an angle, coming back on itself. When she pokes her head into it, she can't see any way through. But the cats are gone. She has to climb up and inside the tube-like shape. She follows it around again before she slides out on the other side. A wider passageway than the one they just left.

"That's amazing." Zada is full of awe and wonder. "Mother would love this place." That brought her down somewhat. But still this sandstone is so warm and beautiful she can't help but love it. It calls joy to her heart.

"Don't worry about your mother. She is already out of the grip of the NiVarian king. His son, Baz, and Avril are on the mountain heading for the first Hearts Rest... Coming this way, but it will take them much longer than your trip took you."

"What is Hearts Rest? I've never heard of it before." She sighs, "I guess it's another secret the Protectors kept. So, what is it?"

"Stone huts, a string of them across a high hidden mountain pass, more treacherous than the Stone Path you took or even the desert. It is older than Stone Path. But still crossable with great care and difficulty, if you're brave, or desperate enough to try it. And they are."

"But how can they cross the desert without a Staff once they cross the mountains?"

"There is another way."

That is all he would say

"How do you know all this?"

"You need to ask?" He looks at her with lifted brows. "After dreaming with our four-legged kin?"

"Oh," Zada felt embarrassed she hadn't thought of that. "Of course."

It was full dark by the time they arrived in the city, Stone Haven. Too dark to see anything more than a vague shape of things. Sinacrib leads the way to a small house cut and carved into the side of the sandstone cliff, a small comfortable place. A kitchen and living space, and a small sleeping room.

"My wife, Kavita, will come in the morning with breakfast." He says goodnight and leaves.

She is so tired that she lays on the cushioned stone bed and closes her eyes, Jag jumps up beside her and they are fast asleep within minutes.

# CHAPTER NINE

*Avril and Baz climb up the steep side of a mountain overlooking Harapo Lake. Holding onto tree branches and protruding roots. They are above the deciduous tree line and into the evergreens as the trees thin far above the ruined gardens and groves of Aggedae.*

*"I have never been up this far." Avril sits down to rest, breathing heavy. "None of the Aggedae have, anyway not in recent history."*

*Looking out to the view of the long string of mountains is breathtaking. The sun slanting to the west, the vivid colors of sunset casting streaks of purples and pinks across the mountain peaks.*

*"I have never seen such beauty," Baz says as they sit down on a flat space to rest, "If you have never been up this high before how is it you know the way?"*

*"I'm sure you've seen Sand Cats before…"*

*"Yes. I know what they are. Our people don't like them or make pets of them like the Aggedaeans do. What do Sand Cats have to do with you knowing the way?"*

*"Something few people know about a Sand Cat is that they see things, they know things. And… They can dream what they know to us who love them."*

*"Dream… Like what we do at night when we sleep, that kind of dream?"*

*"Yes."*

*Baz and Avril are high above Harapo Lake, directly above the palace from where they escaped before dawn. They can hear King Trabot and*

*Mollin calling out his guards. They hear the commotion far below them, but on a clear late afternoon, sound carries.*

*"Well, I guess they have discovered you're gone, that we're gone. It's Mother's birthday today. It's why we had to leave this morning. But I can tell you, they will never look up here. Heights scare them."*

*"No," Avril agrees. "They won't think to look up. It will be dark before long. We need to move on to the first Hearts Rest before nightfall, or we'll never find it in the dark and have to sleep in the open. Even if it's raining. Come on, let's go."*

Zada wakes in the night, thinking about the dream. Her Mother is free. Removing her boots and Tabard, she climbs under her covers dressed in her white pants and long-sleeved tunic, the typical white garments of the Heartsease Keepers and Protectors.

"Baz. The son of a king." What an odd world to wake to. All the shifting keeps life interesting, though. She breaths softly, Jag stirs, but doesn't wake.

* * * * *

Avril is awake, but it is still dark outside the tiny stone hut. She is preparing something for them to eat before they head out for the day.

Baz sits up from sleep, stretching, and yawns. "It's odd," he says, "I dreamt of a girl I don't know, but she has hair like yours, only it is longer."

Avril smiles, "That's my daughter, Zada. We're going to where she is. My Sand Cat was dreaming with her last night, telling her we're alright. Some of it slipped into my dreams, I saw her, too. She has arrived at Stone Haven, where the Lumdie live. Another Heartsease," she waged her head, squinting her eyes, thinking about that statement, "Well, different than ours, yet the same Spirit."

"But how did I see her? Did your Sand Cat cause that?"

"Life is... complex... we often don't understand why or how things come to us. Sometimes they just do." Avril gave a little shrug.

Baz sits in silent thought, "I went to Heartsease when I was just a boy."

Avril, hides a smile, he is still just a boy, verging on a young man, yes, but still a boy, she thinks. By the time they arrive at Stone Haven, if they make it, she suspects he will be a man then, through the trials of the journey.

"Oh, how did you like our Listening Room?"

Baz's eyes take on a faraway hollow look, eyebrows pinched together, a pain etched on his face. "The only person who ever loved me was my Aggedaean nursemaid. She went often to Heartsease, I ask her one day where she was going, and she took me with her. But it had to be a secret, because my father wouldn't have liked that, I went with her on the rare occasion after that first time. He wouldn't have liked knowing I had gone once, let alone more than once. He doesn't believe in the peaceful ways of the Aggadae. He thinks their peaceful ways make people weak."

He is quiet, eating slowly the food he'd packed, but finally he speaks again.

"Vavari loved me as her own. And I loved her like a son loves a mother."

Avril waits for him to say more, listening, hoping to draw him out in the quiet, to continue. She knows there is more. He is silent for so long this time she thinks that is all he is going to say for now. But suddenly he is sobbing, huge wracking grief, he wraps his arms around himself and rocks back and forth.

"They killed her in the public square along with the rest of your people, for the entertainment of a savage court. They hacked, and stabbed, sent the dogs to rip them apart. They forced me to watch. That's when I started planning to set you free." He took in deep shuddering breath, calming himself with a great effort, the tears flowing freely, his hands dashing them away.

"And to go with you, even if they found us both and killed us. It would be better to die with you, than live with them. They are heartless monsters and I refuse to be one of them."

Avril had heard that many of the Aggedae had been killed. She didn't know it was all. She thought it was the Protectors only. That was expected because of things Uddo had said while on guard duty. She takes a deep breath to calm herself, too. Her grief now doubled, the horror of the images Baz must have seen, were more than she could stand… and yet… she still lived.

"They wouldn't spare her, not even when I begged. They called me... *weak*. They said, we'd all be better off without your kind mucking around in our business."

"I'm so sorry. I know her, knew her, she is... was a good person. And Baz, *love doesn't make us weak*. It gives us strength to stand in the gaps of life when things get hard. And there are always hard times mixed in with the good. There are wounds... We can be for others what Vavari was for you when you needed someone to love you. Someone to love."

It will be hard being the last Aggedaean, she thinks, a wound in her heart that might never heal.

"I was never loved until she came to take care of me. My own mother never cared. The third wife of King Trabot, that's what she was to me. I was never even allowed to call him Father or her Mother. Not out loud in the presences of others. She is the most beautiful woman in the kingdom, people say. That's why he loves her and everyone else hates her, that's what the king says. He never had time for me, only time for her."

"Once," he continues, "she became so restless and bored with palace life, that she tore up all her silk robes because she loved to hear the ripping sound it made. It amused her. He ordered more silk to be brought in for her, bolts of it. As costly as that was, she ripped it all to shreds. Bolt after bolt. Piles of shredded silk she cast into the streets for the poor, more an insult than a charity. What would make a person do such a thing?" His breath catches on a shallow sob. "I'm ashamed to know she birthed me."

Avril's heart ached, for him, for herself, for his mother, for the people under such a harsh rule creating poor spirits, dead hearts.

"No child born should ever grow up unloved." Tears were running down her cheeks, too. "Your mother is unhappy. She may never have known one person who loved her. She may never have had a Vavari in her life. She may not know how to love. Not being loved, not loving... twists a person. We might have been able to help her at Heartsease... but..." Avril trails off.

Baz nods his head, wiping his hands across his eyes, a sleeve across his nose. "I know that is true. Vavari told me. I understand it... in a way... and I *don't* understand it. I have never seen her smile. Nor heard her laugh. She has no joy." He shakes his head. "The king only wants to make her happy. He'd do anything to make her laugh. Everything he does is to please her. Anyway, that's what his first wife says. Uddo's mother."

They eat the remaining breakfast in silence, as light begins to stream in the open door. They pack up for their long day ahead.

"Time to go." Outside Avril takes a deep breath of sweet air. "There is a very treacherous narrow ledge we must walk not far from here. I don't think we will be able to stop for food or rest until we are on the other side of it. If you have trouble with heights, don't look down. Not far after this part of the path there is another Hearts Rest hut. I think we will sleep well tonight. At that time Jag will dream me the next part of our journey… One day at a time."

# CHAPTER TEN

Jag's rumbling purr wakes Zada, his face just inches away from hers. "Hey, big guy, what's up with the crowding?" She stretches and rolls onto her back and sits up. "Go, if that's what you're asking." She laughs. "Go find your Ollish." He is off with a bound and out the door.

Zada climbs off the bed and puts on the Tabard and picks up the Staff. In her living space she sees a stone table jutting out from the wall beneath a narrow window, with two wooden stools on both sides. One is occupied by a woman with long black hair and a rosy light brown skin. She is wearing a simple floor length tunic style dress. It is a swirl of bright colors like nothing Zada has ever seen before.

"Good morning, Zada, I'm Kavita, Sinacrib's wife. I have brought you breakfast."

"Good morning."

"I knocked but you must have been asleep. I've put some fruit in the storage box. And this you can eat now."

"Thank you. I love what you're wearing. It's beautiful."

"I make cloth. That's my passion. And sometimes it comes out exceptional. What do you like to do?"

"Hmmm." Zada didn't know how to answer that. "I help Mother with the people who come to Heartsease. I guess that's what I do. I help people."

"That's what we all do. We're all family here. Family helps family," she says, smiling broadly, "But what makes your heart sing?" Kavita stands up. "Well, you think about that, because here you can follow your hearts-desire, you can find your passion, and create what you love."

A small boy comes popping in at the open door, "We're waiting, Momma. We all want to meet her."

Kavita's laugh is warm and cheering. "My son, Iuka."

He comes in, Kavita sits back down, and Iuka climbs onto her lap. "Let her eat something first," she says, smiling.

Zada tries to eat, but after a few bites she realizes she is too excited to wait to meet the people and see the city. "As good as this is... as kind as you are... I don't think I can eat another bite. I want to see your city! Meet your people."

"Your people too. Alright then." Kavita wraps the breakfast and put it in a hole in the wall, that has a small door. That must be the storage box, Zada thinks.

"Yea!" Iuka jumps up and down then takes her hand. "Come on. I'll introduce you."

Outside and down the curving steps, there is a small crowd waiting. "Hello's, and greetings." Come from many smiling faces welcoming Zada to Stone Haven. She is surprised again, because they are a people of every shade of skin. From very dark to very white. Something she did not expect. A shiver of joy runs through her. What a marvelous thing. From young to old. They are a happy, kind people. Just like the stories her mother used to tell her about them, without ever mentioning the variety among them, an unknown thing out in the world as it is, back in Harapo the NiVar don't like differences. They can't tolerate anyone not like themselves. They kill, use or ignore, difference.

Yes. What a marvelous thing. Human dignity displayed in community.

"I am Zada Zan, and I am delighted to meet you."

"Ahh, I'm supposed to do that." Iuka pipes up. And there is good natured laughter among the small crowd.

"Alright, Iuka, introduce us to Zada," a man says.

The boy runs from person to person, shouting out their names. Zada knows it will take her some time to really get the names to the faces, there are so many. But the thing she sees right away is how much love there is among them. They are so easy with each other. Like they are true friends. Family. Like the Keepers and Protectors are... were among themselves.

"The large building there…" Kavita points to a very large building in the middle of the market place. "…is our school, library, and gathering hall. We call it the Heart. Would you like to see it?" Kavita asks. "The stone for the building was cut from where our small lake is now. Not far from here. The building is two hundred and fifty years old. Come."

"Yes. I'd love to see it." Zada answers.

The building is bigger, more beautifully crafted than the palace of King Trabot, back in Harapo. It sits in the middle of the common space, with paths and statues all around it, art of many kinds, and beautiful fountains, and some crystalline stones they call desert diamonds of many sizes, scattered around the gardens. Between the cliff apartments and the building, there is an intriguing fanned-out market place in a half circle. Permanent structures and work spaces.

Once inside the large building, the first room they come to is the library, with many, many scrolls. Racks of them, and tables with people reading or writing.  Another large room with windows letting in the sunlight, has small, low tables, and cushions in front of them. The only school she has seen before has been for adults. "Is this for… children?" she asks. "Your school is for children?"

"Yes. We teach them to read and write." An older woman says. "I'm a teacher… There is much too be curious about in this world. Many things to study."

The woman had flame red hair and green eyes, and skin as white as milk.

"We teach them to think…" Kavita adds, "from the inside, to know for themselves what is right and what is wrong. We teach them principals of debate."

A ruddy faced, tall, thin woman speaks. "I am also one of their teachers. This is a sacred place." She lifts her hands, encompassing the whole room, the building its self.

"I believe you. I can feel it." Zada, takes in this new concept of growing children. "In Harapo, children are not taught, they are worked, many to an early grave." Small gasps of shock come from the crowd. "It was one of the things Heartsease worked at changing, but with little success," Zada admits. "In order for people to change, they have to want it." She walks around the room looking at the art on the walls, art the children make. "I love this place already."

"The gathering hall is used for birthdays, weddings, plays, story times, debates, and resolving disputes." Kavita says, "when such things can't be solved by those involved. Which is rare." There is a murmur of agreement that goes around the group. "Or for any purpose needed really. Sometimes we just come here to dance." Kavita laughs. "Who would like to lead the way to Grandfather Tree?"

One of the little girls with long blonde hair, jumps up and down. "Me. Me. I want to lead the way. I'm Loneeia," She takes Zada's hand and leads the way through the building and out the backside to a flower garden with benches and more fountains. This simple, restful garden is art in its self. A peace, and quietude settles upon Zada, and she breaths deep the sweet scents of many flowers, not unlike the gardens and groves she remembers at Heartsease.

A huge tree stands in the middle of this garden on a small hill. There is something so familiar, compelling, about it. It pulls at her, and the White Staff in her hand. A yearning, rises in her heart, a pull to get even closer. As she comes near, she sees Sinacrib there kneeling next to the Grandfather Tree. This reminds her of Mother kneeling in front of the White Altar the day she left home. He turns and smiles. "Ah, there you are," And stands.

Zada takes a deep breath, something new is about to happen. She can feel it well up in her like a spring come from the Staff, a warmth from the Tabard she wears. "I can feel... I can..." She holds out the Staff and Sinacrib takes it. "Do you willingly relinquish this to the Grandfather Tree?"

"I do." Not really knowing, or understanding, but willing.

Sinacrib held the Staff close to the Tree and the Staff begins to glow in his hand. Zada notices that Jag is sitting next to her, with Ollish on his other side, an inseparable pair already. Even as the Staff glows brighter and brighter and the crowd with her exclaim in wonder, the Tree trunk begins to glow, as well. The two merge and the Staff is gone, joining the Tree. Then she understands.

"This Tree came from my great, great, great, grandfather's Staff, didn't it?"

"Yes. Little sister." He raised his hands in blessing on the small crowd with her. "They are united again in strength and protection of this people. Heart and spirit."

Kavita comes up to stand beside her husband. "Can you relinquish the Tabard as well?"

"Gladly." She takes it off, hands it to Kavita and it begins to wrap its self around the white bark disappearing into the tree trunk, joining it. Zada has never felt so full of the Heartsease Spirit as she does right now. Silence settles on every one there. Even the children.

This, too, is a sacred place.

# CHAPTER ELEVEN

*Avril and Baz watch King Trabot and his third wife celebrating her birthday. Since they had been denied the planned death of the Mother Protector of Heartsease, Baz's mother said she wanted all the signal fires lit in her honor. From one end of the River Harapo to the other, the fires are lit. Every allied leader and their armies rush to the kings' aid and defense, for that is the signal of invasion of the Daggale forces.*

*When they arrive and discover there is no invading army, but instead are laughed at by the third Queen because of their shock and then disgust at going to all that trouble to be rallied that they turned and went home, agreeing among themselves they would not come again when the fires are lit, if that is what the King thinks of his allies. A mere toy for the amusement of a third wife. It is insulting. They wouldn't be played with that way.*

In the morning when Avril and Baz wake, he is quiet, quieter than usual.

"Did you dream last night?" Avril is preparing their morning meal, before starting out on their days journey. "Was it about your father and mother?"

"She laughed!" he shook his head, "She doesn't even understand what she has drawn down on them with that laughter. The one time something made her laugh and it will kill them all and she doesn't even know it. Maybe she doesn't care. But she doesn't understand."

"Nor does the King," said Avril.

"That alliance was hard fought for, and he'll throw it away... for a laugh."

"The Daggale will come. But if the signal fires are lit again in the presence of real danger, do you think the allies will come to save them?" Avril wondered aloud.

"No." He says, barely above a whisper.

They ate in silence as the sun's rays creep in the doorway. Finished, Avril puts their food back in their packs.

Baz stands, turns and shoulders his pack onto his back and goes outside, the path continues northeast, up jagged ridges to where they will find the next Hearts Rest.

Avril puts on her pack and follows, directing their way from behind.

*****

Zada sits at the edge of the lake at the lower-level north end of Stone Heaven. As she is getting to know this stone embraced city, she loves the small lake. She is watching the children play at the shallow edge of what once had been a sandstone quarry. The way they carve the cliff side dwelling is ingenuous. Each building, each home, has ready access to water and easy disposal of waste. She doesn't understand how it works any more than she did back home at Heartsease. She was just happy for the convenience of it.

Iuka and Loneeia are in the water having fun after their time in school. Both children have become her guides and companions as she explores her new surroundings. She doesn't see much of Jag until night.

Jag is off with Ollish most days.

Zada thinking about her mother and Baz. She had the same dream they did, she knew this. How she is so certain is the deep connection she feels with her mother. Jag is the link.

Looking out over the water, she marvels. This place is a miracle of hard work, and hope. The passageway Sinacrib brought her through just days ago, to her new home, widens out into an elongated circle, wide enough to hold twenty-five thousand people, she's told. They had more than doubled in size in the three hundred years. They are careful about births as resources and space are limited. Some of their number live in the communities at the ends of two northeast and northwest passageways, one farming the other herders. It's where Kavita gets her wool, mohair, cotton and flax, and the plants to make her cloth and dyes.

There are many times of celebration during the year when the people come in to the Heart to mingle, and meet, she's told. For now, it is enough for her to meet the people here. The peace and safety, she feels here is unmatched to anything she has ever known.

A dreamy languor surrounds her as she sits on a flat stone at lakes edge. She hasn't felt this way since she was a little girl playing at Lake Harapo with her father.

"Hello," a young man sits down next to her. "I am Timnock, do you swim?"

"Yes. I learned in Lake Harapo. But I haven't found any swim cloths yet like the children wear. I see you are already in yours." She likes what she sees. Tall, broad shoulders, brown silky skin, long black hair. His smile is infectious. Kind brown eyes.

"Well, then, you're in luck because I brought you one of my sisters who is about your size. Have you been to the bathhouse yet?"

"Yes, a lovely place."

"You can change there. Meet you in the water." He grins and dives in.

A bundle is beside her. She picks it up and is in the bathhouse faster than you can repeat, meet you in the water, and changes in no time, and out before Timnock has time to swim half way across the narrow end of the lake.

They play in the water like children. Then sit on the shore of the far side where there is shade and they can watch the children swim and play, close enough to be useful if anyone has trouble.

They talk, getting to know each other. Timnock sculps stone. He helped carve her little home.

Hour's pass, the children get out and go home. Zada and Timnock visit until their stomachs start growling at each other. Laughing he says, "Come home with me. Meet my mother and father and my sister, Oshea. We'll feed you."

\*\*\*\*\*

The days stretched into weeks, weeks into months, while Zada learns the place, the people, their Way. She realizes she's been in Stone Heaven half a year. Her mother and Baz are on the other side of the Aggedae Mountain range, traveling with a band of treaders in metals, selling small tools for blacksmithing and kitchen wears. She and Jag have regular dreams of them and their adventures. They are traveling northwest along a river now. They are in sight of another range of sandstone cliffs, not their own sandstone home, but coming ever closer. Zada longs to see her mother in the flesh, hold her close. At least she can hold her close in her meditations, and her love.

*****

Zada and Jag are at Kavita and Sinacrib's home for dinner, a few days later. "Have you and Ollish had any dream of Mother and Baz lately?"

They both smile, Iuka too. "Ollish even gives me dreams of your mother and brother." The little boy says, "How long do you think it will be, Father, before they get here?" Iuka glances at his parents. "That's what she wants to know," then looks at Zada, "Isn't it?"

"Yes." She laughs softly, affectionately ruffling his hair. "Yes. You are very perceptive. But Baz isn't my brother. I haven't even met him yet."

"Well, that doesn't matter." Iuka confidently announces. "We're all kin here. We all have the same last name. Human."

They all laugh at that, but it lands in her heart like a blooming flower, and Zada knows, it's the truest thing she's ever heard.

"Even Jag and Ollish are kin. Did you know Sand Cats mate for life?" Iuka takes a bite, chews, eyebrows drawn together in thought. "Even Mother Terra, the trees, the lizards and all the other animals, too. The sky, the One who Creates. We're all kin. We belong to each other."

Zada digests this food for thought. What wisdom coming from one so young. She wonders what he will be like as a grown man.

"Maybe another couple of months," Sinacrib says, smiling at his son. "I see you've been listening to teacher Pram. And thinking about things. That's good. That's very good."

They eat in silence, enjoying the food for a while. "This is delicious, Kavita, you will have to show me how to make this." Then adds, "Oh, and thank you for the tunic dress you made for me. I love it, the purple matches my hair."

"You've been trying out different kinds of art forms and skills, has your heart called you to any one thing over another?" Sinacrib asks her.

"Not yet. There is so much to see and do here. Timnock and I are leaving to go to the herder community next week to see the animals and meet his cousin's family. Then to the farmers and come back the northwest passageway. Maybe I'll know more about what I want to do when we come back."

"You and Timnock seem fast on your way to becoming a couple." Kavita smiles, "Do I need to start weaving a wedding shawl?"

Zada blushes, "I like him very much. I love him. But... I'm not sure. Is it the kind of love my mother and father had for each other? That's what I want also." Her hair curtains her pink tinged face. "He hasn't said how he feels."

Sinacrib and Kavita burst out laughing. "You can't tell?" they say in unison. Sinacrib reaches across the table and tips her face up, "He adores you."

"You are the light of his life." Kavita pats Zada's arm. "I'm only surprised he hasn't asked you yet."

# CHAPTER TWELVE

Zada and Timnock are up on the flat-topped sandstone cliffs above the city. He has to go up to check on one of the main water reservoirs. It is stopped up.

"You've seen how it can pour down rain, our ancestors had to figure ways to save up the water and keep us safe from floods. We have safety system that took the first hundred years for us to carve and build. It's more just keeping up with maintenance now... and adding to the new systems as needed. Like with your little home. And what we're adding for Baz and your mother."

"Ah, here's the problem. Debris in the duct. It happens all the time." He uses a pole with a hook on one end and pokes the pole in the duct and pulls out a wad of leaves, needles and twigs. "The wind carries all kinds of things up here. Sometimes it's sand and that's really a mess, I have to close the duct down below and climb into the reservoirs to knock the sand loose, then scoop it out when it breaks free."

"I'm glad it is the easy one, then," said Zada, "It will give you a chance to show me where the Watchers live."

"You want to do that today? Well, we can make it to the closest one, Meradok, is there right now. The Watchers stay for a week at a time, you know."

"Will that be where they will be able to see Mother and Baz come to the Herder Community in the northeast? I thought I heard someone say that's where Meradok was going this time."

"I know the Sand Cats have been dreaming to us that they are getting closer. Do you want to go to the northeast Watchhouse or do want to go back home, pack up and go to the Herder Community again, to wait for them there?"

"Is there a way down to the community from the Watchhouse?"

"Yes, they have Watchers use that house to. They have a way up..." Timnock shrugs, "Or down."

"I'd really like to see it. In all these months I haven't been up here. It is inspiring. Look at the vista. This view is spectacular." She walks close to the edge of the cliff and looks down into Stone Haven. "I can see the top of Grandfather Tree, the lake, the bathhouse. The Heart, the Market Place, the gardens. The people look like ants." She laughs.

Timnock comes and picks her up, swinging her around. "You delight me." Setting her down, slowly, holding her close. She reaches up and kisses him.

"And you take my breath away."

*****

It takes them most of the morning to get to the northeast Watchhouse by a straight path over stone, unlike the twisting passageway on the ground, which takes all day. They have to cross one bridge made of wood to get to the wedge in between the northwest and northeast passageways, before there is another straight walk to the Watchhouse, at the opening of the passageway out to the Herder Community, but hundreds of feet up.

The Watchhouse is carved out of a stone nodule on top of a flat surface. A small main room, with a sleeping niche.

The valley stretching out to the east, many shades of beautiful green grass, Zada draws a deep breath. "I didn't realize how much I missed that wide open green until we went to the two communities, where they have so much of it. It is a feast for the eyes."

"Yes. It does the heart good to gladden the eyes with green." Meradok scanning the land as Watchers do. "They have that lush land because of the river nearby."

His Sand Cat, Rumble, comes out of the shade of the watch house, and rubs up against Zada. He was the largest Sand Cat in any of the communities. The one that was with Ollish when they came to lead her home. She scratches under his chin. He rumbles his appreciation.

"Have you seen any new people out there?" Timnock puts his hand up to shade his eyes. "Any new caravans come through lately?"

"You mean like Avril and Baz?" Meradok nods toward Zada. "Her mother and brother?"

Zada had quit saying he wasn't her brother. Knowing the truth of kinship now. They were out there together, protecting each other, helping each other. Brother by birth or not, she is grateful for Baz. Will forever be grateful. She will embrace him as brother.

"Yes." Timnock laughs. "Exactly."

"Not yet." Meradok, smiles at Zada. "But the dreaming tells us they are getting very close to home."

A peaceful quiet among friends that doesn't need filling, extends. Meradok, breaks it though with, "Rumble dreams me the news that Ollish is about to have kittens."

Timnock and Zada just grin at each other, holding hands. "Mother will be so pleased."

\* \* \* \* \*

On our way back to Stone Haven, Timnock asked, "Have you noticed the purple in your hair is fading?"

"So is Sinacrib's purple, his hair is becoming blacker, Kavita says it is what his hair was like before he took the vows to care for the Grandfather Tree..." Zada glances at Timnock's long black hair, "More the color of yours."

"What do you think it means that you're both losing your purple."

"Well, I was born with it. Mother and Sinacrib came by it with vows. I don't think it means we are no longer to keep and protect the people, the Peaceable Way... but maybe the vows are letting us go a different direction than before, now that we no longer have the Staff and Tabards."

They walk hand in hand over the flat stone toward home, a slow pleasant saunter.

"Have you heard there are people saying they've seen a giant White Dragon rise up out of the Tree when the moon is full?" Zada smiles up at Timnock.

"I've known that story of the Tabards being made from the skin a White Dragon who sacrificed his life to save the kin a thousand years or more ago. But that was a very long time before we came here." He bends and kissed her forehead.

"Maybe he's back."

* * * * *

Two days after the cliff roof walk, Ollish gives birth to six kittens. Four of them are white like Ollish. Two, look just like Jag. Three are male, three are female. Everyone comes to see them. A parade of people all day long, just to see the kittens from a distance, so not to disturb Ollish and the babies. There haven't been kittens in the stone city in a couple of decades. Sand cats are very long lived.

This is a cause to celebrate. There will be dancing in the gathering room tonight. All the cats will come, too. Three other life mated pairs were going to have kittens soon as well. There is something big on the rise. The kin will crowd into the Gathering Hall of the Heart and sleep on the floor with the all the Sand Cats present, maybe to get a glimpse of what is to come.

Maybe it is the White Dragon's return after all.

# CHAPTER THIRTEEN

Avril, and Baz arrive in Stone Haven the next day. Tears of joy stream down Avril's face as she holds Zada, at arms-length, "Oh, daughter, let me look at you." Cupping her face. Wiping away tears. "There were so many times I thought I'd never see you again. Or only see you in my dreams."

"Me too." Zada whispers and clings again to her mother never wanting to let her go.

"This is Baz." Avril pulls him into the circle of two so Zada can see him in the flesh for the first time. "Without him I never would have made it."

"Zada," Baz gives her a hug. "Without her I would be dead now. The Daggale invaded my father's city and they are no more."

"I know." Zada kisses his forehead. "I'm so sorry Baz."

"Without Avril, my true self, my essences would be gone, my body might be alive, but inside I'd be dead. I am your mother's son now, and your brother."

"Welcome to the Kin." Timnock says, "We are all brothers here. Mothers, fathers, sons, sisters, daughters. Friends... Kin. Welcome home."

"Yes." Sinacrib joins in. "Come and rest, eat. We would all love to hear of your adventures, if you have the strength for it after you rest, maybe later today or tomorrow evening. Everyone will want to hear. Not only the Gathering Room will be full, but so will the gardens, we'll open the windows."

"I must see the kittens first." Avril follows them to the Gathering Room, where the bed of kittens, Ollish and Jag, are in a small protected niche with people quietly stopping to admire their six babies.

"Oh, Jag. You've done a right and proper good thing to give the world more Sand Cats." Zada takes her mother's hand, "Oh, my dear girl, I am delirious with joy to be home with you at long last."

After a full evening of speaking with and meeting the people, Zada leads her mother and Baz home. Two new rooms, Timnock, along with others in the community, carved and prepared for Avril's arrival with Baz. Rooms connecting to her small home. She even helped them carve.

There is great rejoicing in Stone Haven. The weeks fly by as everyone becomes accustomed to the new.

Zada and Avril spend time to themselves every day, sitting at the lakes edge, making up for the year they lost being apart.

"This is a beautiful place, the Lumdie have listened well to the dreaming."

"Oh, Mother." Zada touches her mother's hair. "Your hair has turned all white."

Avril laughs, "So has yours, my dear. What do you suppose that means for us? No more purple and lilac." They laugh together, because they don't know what it means. But they do know it's alright not knowing everything all at once.

Then quiet settles over them.

And Listening comes.

The Spirit of Heartsease.

And they See what the world can become, like a dreaming, they see what Mother Terra holds in store for the people. The Kin. *Just as Iuka says, all are Kin! Our last name is Human.*

* * * * *

Zada and Timnock marry, they have three children, two girls and a boy. Baz marries, too, and has four boys. And many more Sand Cats are born. The dreaming is strong in the communities of Stone Haven. Zada, Avril and Baz become teachers, opening the hearts and minds of the young, as the young open theirs to them, as well.

Life is good. Not that life is without its troubles and griefs, a heartache now and then, but day to day, not dwelling on the wounds of life, life is good.

Even though Avril dies many years later, she has seen her seven grandchildren grown with children of their own.

There are public debates between the people from time to time, when there are things that need innovation, creation, and rethinking. They set a topic, and speak to as many points of view on it as they can find, then sometimes they switch positions, it is the way they resolve tuff problems, with enough time and talk, solutions are reached, invention and discovery happen, and the people are blessed.

* * * * *

In the fiftieth year since Zada has come to the communities of Stone Haven the population is more than sixty-seven thousand people now. And the Kin have been called to go out into the world in small groups for the past thirty years. A few families at a time. Always a mated pair of Sand Cats go with them, to establish new communities and live the way of love and of common consent, and debate, bringing the Peaceable Way to the world.

Living together, not to tell people how to live, but to show how communities can be a blessing to each other and become a treasure for all living on Mother Terra.

* * * * *

Zada stands beneath the Grandfather Tree. Her youngest granddaughter and her family are saying good bye.

"We love you, Gram. We always will." Her name is Avril, after Zada's mother. Her husband is Jorin, their four children, Jaric, Tovar, Jinova, after her other grandmother, Avery, after Zada's father. They are going out with the largest caravan yet. Carrying all their paraphernalia, tools, animals, whatever they will need to settle in a new place. The kin all came out to see them off.

"Hugs, Great Grandy." Jinova, only three, her little arms reaching up. Zada squats down and scoops her into her arms, then encircles all of her great grand babies and hugs them tight.

"You listen well, I'll see you in our dreams." The last round of hugs with everyone and then they are leaving. "Oh, Timnock, it hurts to see them go." She wipes tears from her cheeks.

Timnock slides his arm around Zada, and pulls her against his side. "Yes. But we still have each other." He kisses the top of her head, now silver white, "The Sand Cats will show them the way to go, and the places to settle where they might do the most-good in the world."

*If you look for the Lumdie, you may find them living next door to you.*

*You may even be Lumdie and not know it. Kin to Mother Terra, and all living things.*

*Listen to the wing beat of the White Dragon, and dream with the Sand Cats.*

Five hundred years later.

## PART TWO

## CHAPTER FOURTEEN

Nyler never understood why he always felt restless. He always felt pulled to move on. He didn't know what he was looking for, others had left the Communities, but always in small groups before. This time it was only him, but whatever it was, kept pulling him to the next place. Jubilee, his companion Sand Cat would dream a new place, and in the morning, they would head out, searching for the elusive goal.

A year ago, when Nyler left home, at the age of twenty-three, his mother and father had given him an obsidian tear drop on a cord. They had worked it, shaped it, smoothed it. All the while poured their love for him into it.

"This is shaped like a tear," His mother said when they gave it to him, "because it makes us sad that you're leaving us, but we always knew this day was coming. You are called to go out, like many of our ancestors before you, to become discomforted for the good of a new community to be started. They will be your comfort and you will be theirs."

"We know you have to go." Said his father, "We've had the dreams, too. Your dreams, shared with us through our Sand Cats and Jubilee. We know you will make a new community somewhere out in the world when you find where you're going. We know this is important. Vital to you. There are Kin waiting for you."

"Just remember," said his mother, "That out in the world, away from the Peaceable Communities, there will be dark days. When they come you look at this tear drop, and know you are loved and protected. Not just by us, but the very existence of Life itself. Original Love. The Creator of all life, to be loved and to love is the greatest choice you can make."

Nyler held the stone in the palm of his hand, it felt warm, it looked black, he gave an inward shudder considering what he might have to face... Outside. Out there, away from home and loved ones. But the whole purpose to their going out was to bring the Peaceable Way to light for the world at large. So, all could see how it can be done.

"When you hold it up to the light..." his mother said, and he did so, "You can see through it."

It became a golden brown, like tinted glass, but you could see the light shine through it, and radiate out in many directions.

"You may have some dark days," his mother said, "but the light will always shine through them, just like it does with this stone."

"Trust in the Blessing Spirit of the White Dragon, the Spirit of Heartsease, and Stone Haven." His father said. "Of every Peaceable Community from the beginning. Of all that exist to this day."

They had hugged. His mother smelled of the fresh baked bread, the loaves in his backpack. His father smelled of the stone dust of a mason. A stone carver, who taught him to find the life, the shape in the rock.

"I love you." Nyler's embrace was long.

"We'll see you in our dreams." They said, "We love you with our whole hearts."

Everyone in his community had come out to wish him well as he left. Hugs and tears and blessings sent him on his way to his first destination.

And here he was a year later... still moving on. Some mornings he felt so homesick he wanted to turn around and go back. Go home. But then he'd think of their history. Of the Lumdie who built the city of Harapo, at the foot of the Aggadae Mountain Range. Of Heartsease that was, is, and always would be. Of Stone Haven, Zada, Timnock and Jag and all the Peaceable Communities spreading out over Mother Terra to bring peace to a wounded world. How many hundreds of years of history was it since Zada Zan lived? What of their history mattered most?

What mattered now was that a place, a people were calling to his heart, who needed hope, love and dreams. Sand Cat dreams. He knew he *had* to go. If not... he couldn't be true to himself. To the Love that kept calling him foreword. To the union with that Love. To the very fabric of life. *His life*. The warp and weft of it.

And so Nyler moved on, following the dreams, the ones he and Jubilee shared. He thought maybe today he would find the edge of the world, where the ocean met the land. The place he kept seeing in their dreams. Where he could stop moving on. Today or tomorrow. Soon... He could feel it on the changes in the air.

They were in a beautiful valley. Green and lush. Huge trees with deep green and white crowns. These trees scented the air with sweet apples. He and Jubilee walked all day among them. Nyler had never seen an orchard this big before. Its rows were irregular, maybe it was natural. He'd never heard of an Apple forest, that idea made him laugh. The glory of Mother Terra was lifting, joyous. He had seen good and bad on his sojourn during this year away from home.

"You do have a sense of humor Mother Terra." He spoke aloud to the earth.

As dusk approached Jubilee climbed a particularly large tree at the edge of this forest, and Nyler knew he had to climb up too, so he did. In the bowl of branches was a cradle of sorts, he brought out food, they ate and later he made his bed, and they prepared for night. This would be a safe place to sleep. The world was peaceful, quiet except for the frog song going on around him in the wet grass after an earlier rain. They drifted off to sleep by the diamond starlight in the indigo night sky.

*She stood weeping, wailing, a young woman, hands hung limply at her sides, her head fallen back staring at the stars. Desolate. At her feet, cast in the light of a full moon, was a dead Sand Cat, torn to bits by some kind of wild animal. So distraught was the woman, Nyler wanted to hold her, comfort her. Share her grief, lift her burden. What a horrible thing. The heart wrenching sorrow he felt coming from her in waves was almost unbearable to him, to her it must be devastating, her link with the Sand Cat torn asunder in such a brutal way.*

He woke. A moment of confusion, wondering where he was? Then he remembered. They were sleeping in the embrace of an old apple tree's branches. Jubilee, curled against him, still slept. Nyler lay there for a long time thinking about the woman. He ached to comfort her, and knew he would someday, for she was at the end of his destination, at the edge of the world. There was the smell of salt air and death there in this place that called him. But love also called. And hope. Of this he was certain. She would be one of the people in his new community. Her name floated in his mind, like a feather on a fire's current, or carried on the wings of White Dragon wind... Shabda.

In the morning they came to a village by the sea. A small city of cobbled stone streets, and outdoor markets, the smell of fish and cattle, cook fires and wood.

He walked through the streets hoping to see the dark, haired young woman, Shabda. As he went, he checked out the businesses on the one main street. One appealed to his curiosity and he went in. There was an older man behind a table, this shop had a door that would lock and real window glass. He traded all of his small carvings of wood and stone to the man who sold kitchen stone and glass wear, and other odds and ends. His carvings were toys for children, but they seemed to fit what he saw in this place.

"These are exquisite!" the shopkeeper said, turning them over, then turning them again in his hands, Nyler's little animal figures. "What do you want for them?" The older man asked.

Nyler knew the world outside the Communities used coins, but had no idea, even after a year dealing with the concept, what they were worth to this man.

"Well, how much can you give me for them?" He knew if he got coin, he could exchange them for food at the booth down the way.

"Umm, well... I think I can give you ten coppers for the lot of them."

"How much food will that buy at the stand down the way?"

"Not enough, he's over-priced." The man, squinted his eyes at Nyler, held his hand out, and shook hands with him, "My name's Burwick. You should be able to live on that amount for several weeks, young man.

Where were you raised that you don't know the value of money? Or of the work you do?"

"I came from a Community that only does trade, so we have no need for coin. No one goes hungry or homeless. We all work. We take care of each other, like family. Not like I've seen in some places."

"Well, I'd like to visit your home. It must be a very special place, but here in Sea Side, we use coin, so you need to learn it's value, or your talent and good nature will be taken advantage of." Burwick said. "You seem almost too innocent for this world, boy."

Nyler laughed, "You may be right. I'm Nyler. It's good to meet you, Burwick."

"Are you going to be around for a while. I think these will sell quickly to the Sea Side travelers, if you have more or can carve more, I'd be glad to keep you in coin."

"It's what I love doing. Wood and stone speak to me. So, yes," Nyler smiled.

"You're different somehow, not like anyone I've met." Burwick looked him over thoughtfully. "Be careful here. There are some bad people, rough men, some women, too, that would rob you blind, given half a chance. Don't you let them!"

Nyler smiled again. He knew that was the truth. He'd met some of them in villages and small towns all year long. He knew how to spot them, now, and avoid them, *most of the time.*

"I know." He said, and rubbed a purple scar above his left eyebrow. "Thank you for being one of the good people."

Burwick laughed, "You *are* a strange one. Don't go to that first food booth," He waved his hand in front of his nose, "His food is bad. Go down to the third one, her name is Liska. Tell her Burwick sent you. She'll give you a good deal. An honest deal." The man was setting the little figures out on shelves for people to see through the windows. "She may be able to point you in the direction of cheap lodgings, too."

"Well, thanks," Pocketing the coin, Nyler reached across the counter and shook hands with the older man again. "I'll be back when I carve more, is there any animal you're partial to? I can do almost any animal I've known."

"What about that cat you have with you."

"Jubilee?"

"That's the biggest pet cat I've ever seen. Long legs, huge paws, big ears. He's more like a medium size dog. How did you ever get him to follow you around like that? Like a dog." Burwick shook his head amazed.

"*She's* a Sand Cat." Nyler squatted down and gave Jubilee a scratch under her chin, she lifted her face and stared at Burwick as if she had understood what he'd said about being like a dog. "And she isn't as big as some Sand Cats. She's only about thirty pounds. I can carve her with my eyes closed. She's been with me since I was a child." Nyler looked up at Burwick. "I can do as many of her as you'd like. Wood is quicker, but I can do stone, too. If it's the right kind."

After buying enough food to last at least a week, Nyler and Jubilee found an overgrown path up the side of the high hill at the edge of the city next to the ocean beaches. The harbor not too far away, where Liska said he could find fresh fish for Jubilee.

"I bet we could get a gorgeous view from up there on top of those cliffs, Jubilee. Maybe we can find a spot up there to camp, somewhere away from the noise and bustle. Somewhere I can think, where we can dream, where I can work."

Nyler knew Jubilee couldn't talk, but sometimes he felt he could almost hear her thinking. He wondered for the thousandth time how they could dream together, he was sure other animals couldn't dream with people. And he knew perfectly well, that Jubilee knew, that he knew, what the dreams meant, too, most of the time. It was a communication, a connection he never fully understood, he just lived in it, accepted it as truth. He had seen it lived out to the image, too many times, not to believe the truth of it. Like answered prayer, messages from the White Dragon. Jubilee was like his own guardian life guide. It was the way all the Kin felt about the Cats.

He thought of the young woman, from the dream last night. Was that how she felt about her Cat? Did she feel like the loss of her guide and guardian had crushed her spirit? How would he have felt if that had been Jubilee? Was Shabda here? In this city? It was too dark in the dream to tell, even with the moonlight, but there was the smell of the sea, of fish, and damp ocean air, like in this city. It felt right. For the first time, it felt right… Almost.

Jubilee led the way. The path went up the steep hillside, switch backed through the trees and rocks, snags and open spaces. Wide places to rest, where they could've camped, but Jubilee wouldn't stop for long. They kept going till they were near the top at the edge of the cliff side. There he found a plateau... and a cave, a blessed cave... Well, Jubilee found the cave. A home with a perfect view of the city and the ocean. A blue-green sea, a gem of shifting shadows of light and dark.

Nyler set up camp, "You found us the perfect place, Jubilee. A stone home, and no landlord but Mother Terra." He rubbed his hands together, warming them by the fire he built toward the back of the cave, out of the wind, dispelling the clammy dampness, a small chimney crack let the smoke escape into the air outside.

A short time later, they sat outside and watched the sun set to the left of what he thought of as his front yard, the ocean caught fire with vermillion and flashed with gold as it sank into the sea. Nyler hoped Jubilee would send this image home to his parents, to the whole Peaceable Community. All of them. Such beauty should be shared.

This was true coin.

# CHAPTER FIFTEEN

*Nyler was carving his name and Jubilee's on a flattish stone inside the entrance of the cave. The stone was large, white, and fairly smooth. "Our lintel stone." It sparkled in the fire light. It would be easy to engrave on its surface. Chisel and mallet, he worked their names into the stone. Nyler. Jubilee.*

*After he finished, he noticed other names. Below his name and Jubilee's were five names. He didn't remember carving them, but there they were.*

*Then he realized, "This is a dream."*

*Shabda*

*Jack*

*Jandy*

*Winshaw*

*Ashling*

*He didn't know those people... yet. But he was convinced he'd carve those names... all of them, when he would wake up. He knew they were his people. The ones who called to him on the wings of the White Dragon's wind. The breath of Spirit. The dreams of a Sand Cat.*

The cave was tall enough that he could stand up in it, without touching the ceiling, even when he stretched on his toes, reaching up. On closer inspection with his fire built up, he could see it was large enough to home a small crowd with room to spare. He was unusually tall, and thin. His lanky frame fit easily in his new home. Even through the entrance which was only a skinny slit in the rock. If he hadn't known stone as well as he did, and have a Sand Cat who disappeared into the entrance, he might have missed it all together, not seen it in the dimming light last night. He stoked the fire, and looked for the stone he had seen in their dream. Jubilee was already out hunting, he supposed, so Nyler unpacked his stone carving tools and set to work carving their names. Not knowing who they were yet, but he knew they were the beginning of his community. Where ever they were, whoever they were... They were Kin.

Shabda – The woman he had seen in his dream the night before last.

Jack

Jandy

Winshaw

Ashling

Nyler made the names beautiful with curled, embellished sweep. A stone testament for when he found them. Shabda, the only one he had a vision of, and that only by moonlight. He worked all day on the white stone inside the entrance of his new home, he took breaks as needed, he sat outside loving the view. Nyler had seen large bodies of water before on his travels, but this was his first real ocean. It was magnificent, appearing endless, the horizon line curving away into sky. It filled him with awe. It sang of Love with its shushing tides, as it retreated and power with its crashing waves at the base of the hills when it came in at the edge of the cliffs and the city. The curved bay and harbor with ships in port. Things he had heard of but never seen, till now. Travel showed him the hugeness of life, the different ways people lived. The judgements people made on assumptions. The fear, hate, lack of trust. It was heart breaking. He *knew* it didn't have to be that way.

He missed the Peaceable Communities. The Way of Peace.

The next day Nyler found some sand stone, good for carving quickly, he smiled, "Sand stone for a Sand Cat," and a few downed branches of teakwood outside the cave close by. Teak is a hard wood but not difficult to work with, and set to it, as he wondered about the five people. And by evening, he had a stone image of Jubilee. By the next two days, a wooden figure of Jubilee joined the stone one. This wooden one was bigger than the stone, she sat and washed her paw. Nyler turned the small figure in his hands, and smiled. This was good work. Maybe better than usual. Easy, as he loved his subject and the pungent wood scent that came with the carving inspired him.

The next one was even larger. He felt more than satisfied with his work. Three good representations of Jubilee. And even though he still had food he could eat, he wanted to go down to the city and see if he could find any of his five people. Maybe Burwick or Liska might know them. He could trade his statues and buy more food before coming back.

He left, without Jubilee, she often spent time by herself while he went about business of his own. It took him most of the morning climbing down the path. His three carvings wrapped in a cloth in his backpack. He had left most of his things in the cave, not worried that anyone would find them. All of his heavy tools, for wood and stone, he left under the guard of a watch Cat.

"Well, there you are!" Burwick said as he entered the shop. "I thought I'd see you back here in a few days. Did Liska tell you where to go for a good bed, and a hot meal?"

"Oh, no, I'm more comfortable on the ground. I'm camped out up the hill." He waved toward the west side of the city. "Ready supply of wood and stone up there." Nyler said, and nodded his head toward the window shelf. "It looks like you were right. Over half of the figurines are gone. I'm glad to see you didn't waste your coin."

Burwick, waved his hand at Nyler, "Are you kidding? You really don't know your own worth. Your own talent, do you? It's rare. You're good with your hands. True flare is hard to find these days."

Nyler only smiled, knowing he was good at what he did, but not wanting to be boastful. Loving something like the smell of wood, and the rough chips of stone accumulating at his feet, the form of something emerging in his hands, was always the reward. The meaning. The gift. Mind and hands giving birth to something new. Something that hadn't been before it was. Something emerging from stone or wood, a whisper coming to voice. Then sharing it. Back in the Communities, he gave these small carvings away. All the children had a carving of his. One, or two or more.

Thinking of Community gave him a flash of the night time vision, of the woman he had seen, so sure of her name. "Do you know a woman by the name of Shabda?" Nyler asked. "Dark hair, about so tall." He held up his hand to about his shoulder. "Maybe she had a Sand Cat, like my Jubilee, too. A big black Cat? Some kind of animals killed him. Have you heard of anyone like that?"

Burwick's bushy brows creased, "That's a shame. But I've never seen any cat like yours before anywhere." He shook his head slowly, "No. I don't think I have heard of anyone by that name. It means Truth. Or the Word of Truth. Something like that."

"Word of Truth." Nyler repeated. "That's beautiful."

"Shabda." Burwick still shaking his head. "No, I know of no one by that name. I'm sorry I wish I could help you. Go to Liska, often a woman might know another woman, where a crusty old man like me would not."

"I'm looking for four other people too. Jandy, Winshaw, Ashling, and Jack."

"Jack? What kind of name is Jack?" Burwick gave a sigh, and chuckled. "What do you have for me?"

Nyler pulled out the three carved Jubilees and Burwick was delighted. Trade completed, coin in pocket, he left the shop and walked down the cobbled street to Liska's booth.

He picked up more fruit, vegetables and grain and fresh baked bread. Liska didn't know any of the names he had carved in the white stone. So, he went back home and met Jubilee on the path going up.

"I hope your hunt was more productive than mine."


Nyler carved, and searched. This was the first time he'd ever not found what was in his dreams. The location was correct. He knew this with a certainty. But the people... he had only seen the girl... young woman. The others were only names. People unknown to him. When he asked about them, he couldn't even give descriptions of them. Nothing... no ages, or what they might look like. And just like Burwick, people would say, "What kind of name is Jack?" He could only give a description of Shabda, and that was limited.

Maybe they were traveling to this place. How could he leave to go look for them? And if Jubilee could see more... she wasn't giving it to him. He had never known frustration like this before. He was being called, but *couldn't* move on. This *was* the place! He was sure of that. The call was strong, the place was right... and yet. The one word hovered in his mind, every day. "Wait."

He did ten more carvings, went down into the city a couple of times a week. He had almost lost hope, when he had an encouraging dream from his parents. Things were going as usual back home. His cousin was getting married. He fingered the obsidian tear drop on the cord around his neck. Remembered what his mother and father had said, what felt so long ago, now. All these dream images made him homesick again. Even so, as they bedded down, he hoped for another one, a dream of home, loved ones and comfort.

*He stood on the overgrown path. Holding his breath. Two of the largest hounds he had ever seen, were blocking his way down the path. Growling, deep throated sounds of slavering threat. They would kill him, he thought. Suddenly he knew they were what had killed Shabda's Sand Cat. These two were big enough and savage enough to take down a full-grown man, and tear him to bits, as well as any Sand Cat. They were twice the size of the biggest Cat he'd ever known.*

*Then Jubilee jumped from the hillside to the path between him and them, hissing and growling, spitting and slapping at the hounds like a wild thing ready to attack. Jumping on the path to save him.*

"Nooooo!" Nyler woke, and sat up screaming that one word. He buried his face in his hands and wept. This couldn't be. Couldn't be. Must not be. Jubilee woke up and gave him a head butt. He wiped his face and Jubilee licked the tears from his hands and cheeks, her rough, and raspy tongue against his skin. She added a chirruping purr of comfort. This was the scariest dream he'd ever had. A dark dream. He would pack up this morning and leave this place. Go down to the rooming house Liska had told him of each time she saw him. She worried about him. And now he was worried about Jubilee.

Was anything worth losing Jubilee over? But there she was, a foot from his face staring him in the eye. An intense stare. A knowing stare. So, what did it mean? What did she know that he did not? "Just because you had a dream, *didn't mean you always knew the outcome."* He remembered his father saying once. Even though that had always been his experience before. He would pack up and go find a room in the city. At least that way Jubilee would be safe. He hadn't seen any hounds like those down in the city. Ever. Maybe that would be enough. Maybe they were only in the hills. Was this dream a warning only... was he jumping to conclusions? Making assumption of his own?

Fear came creeping on sly feet. He knew sometimes bad things could happen. And he couldn't let fear hack at the cords of Perfect Love. He couldn't let fear rule. Not if he was to find his people. But he couldn't help wonder if anything happened to Jubilee, how would he ever find them. He closed his eyes and pulled Jubilee onto his lap, under his chin. She began to purr.

# CHAPTER SIXTEEN

Backpack and bedroll, all his gear packed, he was loaded up, and on his way headed down the path in a wispy fog that curled thickly about his legs unlike anything he had seen so far here at ocean's edge. Every now and then he could see Sea Side below. Hear the sounds of a place waking up, drifting on the still, fog muffled air. Jubilee was above him to his right in the under growth keeping pace. He couldn't see, or hear her, but he felt her presence there beside him. Good. He thought, she's coming with me this trip, better she stayed out of sight though... but this was so like his dream it made him shudder with unease.

On the path ahead the air simmered in a way that mystified him, it made him feel weird. It shifted, shimmered, illuminated in an unnatural kind of white, blue and pink light. It went all the way up the hill to where Jubilee was moving silently in the underbrush. It was almost too bright to look at directly. He held his hand up to shield his eyes.

The first deep growl, raised the hair on the back of his neck and froze him in place. The second one made the hair all over his body lift and goose flesh rise. The third growl, and the fog cleared a bit and he saw them. The two monstrous hounds from his dream, just below him on the path at the bend on the switchback. He took a deep breath, and stepped through the shimmery mist, Jubilee jumped between him and the two hounds.

"Noooooo!" he screamed, and ran toward them waving his arms wildly. The two hounds were running toward Jubilee. She took a flying leap over the cliff edge. Nyler watched her drop, and disappear into the leafy crown of a teakwood tree below. The hounds went flying after her. Dropping down the cliff side. Yelps and barks, a growl... a whine, then silence. The tree branches and leaves the only movement.

"No, no, no, no, no." Nyler slid in his hurry down the path that seem more over grown than usual, the over growth clutched at him but he kept going, tearing through the brushy path. "No," he kept saying. Until he got to the bottom of the of the switch back, some thirty feet below, to an open space on the trail. "Jubilee!" he yelled looking everywhere.

There she sat, cleaning her paws, her face, her tail. Relief flooded Nyler. Bent over hands on knees he caught his breath, with a grateful huff of laughter. Then he saw the hounds.

Next to Jubilee was a dead, twisted hound, laying draped over a bolder, his back broken. A bloody tongue lolling from its mouth. The other hound not far away, was impaled on a snag. A stench rose from the bodies that echoed the appalling sight of the dead hounds. An awful, evil smell that made him want to gag.

"Oh, Good Mother Terra." Nyler ran to Jubilee, fell to his knees. "You could have shown me this. Why did you have to scare me like that?" She only meowed and rubbed against him with a sibilant sound, looked up at him like that was the only way it could have happened. As if to say, you had to learn not to assume, and you had to follow me.

How could he defend them from animals like that? If there were more of them. Such huge, terrible beasts. Vile Cat killers. Nyler thought of Shabda and her Sand Cat. He knew what terror she must have felt. He wondered if she had seen it happen, or only found him after. He wondered if these had been the animals who had killed her Cat?

Then he noticed the fog had cleared. Gone... Completely gone. As if it had never been, into a bright, clear day. And what he saw before him down in the city below was... *Wrong*.

*Very wrong*. The city was in silent ruin. He had seen ruins before in his travels. But how could this be? And the city was so much bigger than it had been only minutes before. It curled around the beach and down it, and into the apple tree valley. Ruins of impossibly tall skinny buildings reaching into the sky above the hills on either side of the city, like broken fingers pleading with the sky.

*What was this?*

He felt confused, dizzy and at a loss for understanding of what he was seeing. Then he noticed a child, and a Sand Cat below him on the path's next switch back.

"Hello, she said. "My name is Ashling?"

"Ashling..." He felt dumfounded as he stared down at her.

"This is Jump." She said, "He showed me where to find you."

"Oh," he stared stupidly. "What happened here?"

"War." She came up the path, knelt down and stroked Jubilee. "Thank you for getting rid of those last two Hedge Hounds. They've killed enough of you Dream Cats." The child said to Jubilee. "It's nice to finally meet you face to face." The child smiled up at Nyler. "And you too."

Nyler felt astonishment wing through his whole body in a frisson as he realized what the girl had said her name was.

Ashling stood up, "Come on, the others are waiting. We shouldn't be out here for long. The looters come into the city in the mornings. Be quiet. If you see anything, or anyone else. Any kind of movement, stop and hide until I say go. Got that?"

Numbly, Nyler followed Ashling and Jump, Jubilee trailing behind him for a change. They seemed to walk for hours, through rubble and collapsed buildings. Hide, then dash. He didn't recognize any part of the city he had walked through just a few days ago. He couldn't understand what had just happened.

Nyler noticed as they went, they were getting closer to a street and what looked like a few buildings that were intact, more or less. There was a balcony on the third house on the left side of the building, he could see people gathered there watching them arrive. One, he thought looked like it might be Shabda. He hurried his pace, "Is that Shabda?"

"Yes." Ashling quickened her pace to almost a run, "And Jack, my brother, Winshaw, and his girlfriend, Jandy." She ran laughing, up the broken walkway, "I found him!" She yelled. "I found them. *The last two hounds are dead*. Jubilee tricked them."

Nyler saw Shabda collapse. A big barrel-chested man caught her and sat her in a chair.

Still confused, but knowing he had finally arrived home, he had reached family. Nyler ran after the child, Ashling.

*****

Seven houses were tucked away in the crease of a canyon, barely visible from the broken streets below. The streets were made of some odd continuous stone he'd never seen before. Ashling called it concrete. These *homes* were mostly protected from the main view if you were in the bay, or the city ruins. They called it a housing development. A suburb. They were all very large buildings, like palaces. Shabby palaces. Broken, ruined palaces. He thought many families must have lived in these large buildings.

"The reason we still have electricity is because of the solar panels." Ashling's brother, Winshaw, explained as a greeting. Nyler had no idea what that meant, but he thought the boy was maybe fourteen or fifteen. Jandy was a pretty redhead, with the greenest eyes, he had ever seen.

"Jack was a fireman," Ashling announced, as if that was something Nyler, was supposed to understand. Jack was a big man, as tall as Nyler himself, but with muscles everywhere. He had a beard that was half way down his chest. Braided. Beards Nyler had seen before, he had a scruffy one himself, but never braided. He looked around in amazement at the clothes they wore. And the shoes. The only Sand Cat he saw was Jump. And his Jubilee. Were there more?

"Jack took us in after our folks couldn't be found," Shabda said, a sad expression on her tan face. Up close he could see her eyes were a most unusual light sky blue, piercing. Nyler remembered her weeping, and his heart swelled with compassion for the loss of her huge black Sand Cat he'd seen in his dream.

"Actually, *they* saved me." Jack said. "...after my wife was killed in the war."

There was the bit of a babble with everyone talking all at once. Then the big man settled them all down.

"My wife was a doctor… a healer," Jack said, at Nyler's stupefied expression, no doubt.

"A healer…" Nyler looked from face to face. "That I understand. But what is elec - tricity?" Nyler asked fumbling with the word.

They all looked at each other funny. "Did I ask the wrong question?" He frowned. "Where I came from there was no… elec – elec - tricity." He stumbled over the unknown word again.

Jandy frowned then, "Could he be from another time?" She looked at Winshaw, "Or a different planet. Look at his clothes. How odd they are."

Nyler took a step back, looked at the girl, a frown on his face. "Different time? Another Planet?" Nyler looked down at his cloths, it was true they were different, shook his head, his frown deepened. "What are you talking about? It's your clothes that are strange."

"She reads too much science fiction." Winshaw said, in apology.

"Science what?" Nyler scrunched up his face, "What is scie…"

Ashling took Nyler by the hand and led him through a doorway off the balcony, all the others followed, into the large open room and closed the door firmly. She made a click noise and the room was alight. Nyler exclaimed in surprise and wonder. Lights in the ceiling. Light in lamps on tables, lamps that weren't oil. Light. Light everywhere he looked.

"Electricity!" Ashling smiled. "Science. Electricity." She said again, as if explaining something to a toddler, and swept her arm around the room to make it clear. Then flicked the click off, and the lights went out, and they all stood in the dim room in silence for a minute. Then Ashling made the noise of a click and only one lamp was on.

"We don't turn the lights on unless the drapes are closed tight. We don't want anyone to see our light down the streets. The looters."

"In fact, we usually only turn the lights on when we're in the basement," Shabda sniffed, "Looters were the ones with the Hedge Hounds. They hate the Dream Cats. They think they are aliens that want to control human minds. To make us docile and without the killing urge."

The excitement he felt about electricity, drained away, replaced by a deep grief, that anyone would, could hate these animals enough to kill them, to want them dead because of a false belief that Sand Cats wanted control. What kind of place was this?

"But Sand Cats are a blessing, they don't do harm, they don't force anyone to think a certain way… They share dreams, love. Visions in the night to bring us to Community and Kinship. To break the bonds of hate and violence, yes... But…"

Ashling nodded her head, a tear slipped down her cheek. "We know that." She said so quietly, that Nyler barely heard her. "I saw them sic a Hedge Hound on a Dream Cat a little boy was trying to save…" she bowed her head, her long hair hiding her face, Nyler could feel the tears as they came, even if he couldn't see them. "That little boy loved that cat. He fought so hard to save her... But they both... they both... were..."

"Stop it. No more." Shabda wailed. Silence descended on the room again, but this time it was full of awful dread. "I see it every day, my Jarin being torn apart. With nothing I could do. That will be with me forever." A dry sob, "I know we have all suffered. That was something you should never have seen, Ashling. It wasn't right that it happened at all, that dear, sweet boy and his Misha... but we don't have to talk about it... not ever again."

"No!" Nyler spoke quietly, "We do have to remember, have to tell our stories. Have to celebrate the lives we've lost. Honor them with remembering. Otherwise, we never heal." He went to a chair and settled into it.

"Where I came from..." He looked over at the redhead, Jandy, "Where I came from, we have ceremonies that honor our loved ones." Now he set his gaze on Ashling, then Shabda, "We all tell stories about them, some serious, some funny, some sad. But we remember them. Then we have a ceremony of ash and cast their ashes to the winds, or bury their remains, however they expressed their end should be. We honor them. We love them still. And give their bodies back to Mother Terra to care for. But what has lived inside them, the White Dragon carries to the Land Beyond After. Where they are not alone."

By the time he finished they were all sitting on the furniture listening.

"We can do that for everyone you've lost. Human or Sand Cat."

"I'd like that." Ashling sniffed. "I'd like that a lot. We lost our parents. We have all lost so many." She frowned and straightened her shoulders, "Why do you call them Sand Cats?"

"Well..." Nyler stopped, he wasn't sure. "I think it's because they first came to us from the desert. Anything that could live in the desert was exotic. The Sand Cats have been with us for thousands of years. Now they live in all kinds of landscapes. So, I'm not really sure why we call them Sand Cats. Other than, that is what they've always been called."

Then he told them briefly of the history of the Peaceful Lumdie. Of Heartsease, Stone Haven and the blessings of dreaming with the Cats.

"Sand Cats, or Dream Cats... They are our companions, our Kin. They chose to live with us and make our lives better. They bring us together as family. Jubilee has led me here to be with you. Evidently Jump has shown you my coming or Ashling wouldn't have been there to meet me. Your lives have been calling to me for a long time now. We are to build a Peaceable Community here."

"We are to be family!" Winshaw grinned. "I knew something big... Huge, was coming. Even though we only had one Dream Cat, Sand Cat," he shrugged, "I had a dream and saw Jump and Jubilee as life mates. And now that I see her, I know she is exactly who I saw in the dreams."

"Now that the hounds are gone, it will be safer for them." Jandy added.

"Come, time to go down in the basement. It's getting dark out, and even with the curtains drawn, the light seeps around the edges. Down in the kitchen and great room no light can be seen out there at all."

"We'll show you your room." Jack said, as they all moved down the stairs to a large open room with a kitchen on one side, with doors off the wall by the stairs. "You will have to bunk with Winshaw and Me." Jack said, "Sorry, I snore."

"Us girls have our own room." Ashling announced. "Win, sometimes keeps watch from the roof, if we know the looters are in the area. Then he sleeps in the day... when Ja..."

"When I'm not snoring." Jack laughed. The kids joined in the laugher.

These were good people. It was good to feel a free breath with family again. At home... even though Nyler had a lot to learn, it was good to feel safe, warmed among people who loved each other. That caring, that was the heart of home.

# CHAPTER SEVENTEEN

"Ny" Ashling asked some weeks later, "How did our Cats know they were life mates, when none of us believe you two came from our time? How did they dream to each other... and us? Is time like an ocean we're all floating on?"

"Well, I'm not sure I *can* explain that, I'm not even sure what time is after what's happened. I know this is a different place than where I came from. Well not a different place... exactly." Nyler sighed, "You all may be right about this time thing... But what is time? What may be a wall for some, might be a doorway for others, ships on an ocean, that bump and transfer passengers, on the Sea of Time. Whatever it is, looking back on it, I knew the morning we met, I walked through some kind of doorway. Past from one deck to another. And if that was a shift in time. It is what needed to be for us to become family."

Nyler had thought a great deal about this. Wondering if it could work in reverse. Could they go back. Could they find that doorway... Could he take them home with him? He had had no dreams of his family since he came here. Did that mean whatever kind of doorway it was, was now closed? He wondered if the Peaceable Communities still existed in the now of time? Or only the then of time. If there was a wall between them, as he said, it must be what needed to be. But he missed his parents and the Communities, all of them he had known. And he wondered, if this time, this place could devolve into such a horrible whole world war, and wreck such destruction, did that mean they had failed in the past to bring peace to the people of Mother Terra? Was the world so broken its people couldn't be mended? Had hate and violence won? He couldn't accept that.

Here was a child with a fresh heart. One of Love and Hope. He had to believe it was not so, for her, for them, all of his new family. He held his stone tear up to the light seeing the light shine through it.

"What's that?" Ashling reached out to touch it. "It's shaped like a drop of water. Where'd you get it?"

"My parents made it for me," a sad smile softened his face, "The day I left home they gave it to me. It reminds me… where ever they are in time… in or out of this world... that they love me. That I am loved. And even if there are dark times…" That made him grin, "You will always be able to see the light shine through my tear drop… and the dark days."

"I like that!" she said. "Like the ceremony we did for all our lost loved ones. Those were really dark times, but then you came and showed us the light of the people who loved us, and that we still love. That they are inside us, and always will be as long as we remember them."

"Yes, whatever time is, it holds us all in that embrace. We may grieve together, but the remembering can be sweet, the very thing that saves us from despair."

"Like you came here… from then to now… when you transferred ships, or went through the door, where do you think our loved ones went when they transferred from here? Do you think there is another place? A place where they are in a Peaceable Community waiting for us to join them?"

"That is a beautiful thought, Ashling. You have a strong heart and a good brain. And yes, I think they go to the Land Beyond After."

"Yes... the Land Beyond After." she said. They sat there together in the afternoon quiet for some time, enjoying the sun on their faces, a cool breeze. Companionable. Finally, she spoke again.

"Ny… "She grinned, and said in a sing song voice. "I know something you don't."

"Really? Probably a lot of things. What?"

"Shab likes you. I'm surprised Jub hasn't dreamed it to you. She and Jump have been dreaming it to the rest of us for a while now."

Nyler felt chagrined that he and Shabda were being dreamt about. He knew she liked him, but she was shy and he was awkward when they were around each other. He already knew his love for her was different than his love for the others. He was working it out. This child was giving him a kick in the pants, as Jack would say.

"Oh, I have to go help in the kitchen," she jumped off the balcony railing and ran inside, "Here she comes," she sang softly, over her shoulder on her way indoors.

Nyler laughed and waved Ashling on as Shabda came up the steps from the backyard, her arms full of vegetables from the garden, nearly spilling them.

"Oh, here let me help you." They nearly collided, as he took half of them out of her arms. The frisson of touch passed through him with a pleasant little shock. They held a long gaze before the flush came to both their faces. She was beautiful to him, silky long black hair, high cheek bones, bowed lips and those pale sky-blue eyes that melted his heart right down to a puddle on the ground. He could almost never say anything sensible to her when they were together.

"Come on let's go help with dinner." She said, and smiled, ducking her head.

*****

That evening after dinner had been cleared away and dishes done. Winshaw went up to the roof to keep watch.

Nyler thought it was a perfect night for a walk in the hills behind the house. The moon was high, a sliver away from full, Shabda had her dark coat on, he took the opportunity to grab his from the hook by the door, "Would you like to go for a walk," he asked her. "We can go up the hill behind the gardens. I bet there are places where we can even see the bay from there."

Her face was curtained with her long glossy black hair. He could barely hear her soft response, "Yes. I'd like that."

They climbed the green hill to a stand of old apple trees. "This whole valley used to be full of apple trees." She said with a sigh. "Now these might be the only ones left. We pick them. Eat them as desert." She laughed softly, not wanting the sound to carry far on such a clear night.

"I know." he whispered, "When I came to Sea Side, I walked through the valley, it was full of the most beautiful forest of apple trees. Jubilee and I even slept in one…" He paused. "I had my first dream of you that night."

They sat down with their backs to the trunk of an apple tree.

"I knew you were coming… we all did." Shabda looked out over the crumbled city to the bay. "That was before… before Jarin was… killed. He dreamt with me about your coming. Then he…"

"I know that was hard. I kept thinking how I would have felt if it had been Jubilee." He took her hand awkwardly, "I grieved with you that night. I saw you standing in the moonlight, with Jarin at your feet."

"That was not far from here. Right down the hill on the other side." She gave a shudder, and he drew her closer. "I felt what you felt." He put his arm around her shoulders and she leaned her head on his chest. "I know you will always miss him. But I have good news. There was a Sand Cat he mated with just before he… He was actually drawing the Hounds away from her… Mirra. She is coming with more Cats. Jubilee has been dreaming with her lately. She's bringing three new people with her… And she's going to have kittens. Jarin's kittens."

Shabda looked up into his eyes, "Oh!"

Nyler couldn't help himself. He had to kiss that perfect circle of her mouth.

"Oh!" she said again, at the end of the kiss. Then she kissed him.

They spent a good part of the night sitting at the base of that old apple tree, talking about their lives before. The paths that brought them here to each other. A deeper bond was forming tear by tear, laugh by laugh, word by word, story by story. It was good.

*****

A week later a black man and his young son, and a woman were found by Ashling and Jump not far from home base. There was a beautiful soft grey, long haired Sand Cat with them, round with kittens to come, near to bursting. This was Mirra, Nyler saw a glow about her. A soft light of love and good will towards all of these new people.

"Those kittens need a quiet, safe place to be born." Ashling said as she led them up to the balcony. "This is Dr. Shummar, his Cat, Simi. His son, Colby, his Cat Moonda, and Kadora. Kadora was Dr. Shummar's nurse in his office before everything went…" Ashling lifted her hands, spreading her finger in a motion of explosion, along with the sound effects. "Kablooy."

Greetings, welcome and introductions went around.

"Jack, Jack the fireman?" Kadora asked, her short blonde curls bobbing. "The fireman who saved twenty-one people in that office building downtown that burned three years ago, just before the bombs began to drop?"

"Well, I didn't do that by myself." Jack said, laughing. "I had a good number of men and women with me, you know."

"Yes, he's *that* fireman!" Jandy said with a proud grin. "He saved, Winshaw, Ashling and me. And Shabda." She thumbed her chest. "Well, not from the office building, but one of the bombs fell near my house, we were there watching a movie," she frowned, "With popcorn. I really miss popcorn."

Jandy shook her red head as everyone laughed. "Hey, popcorn was my favorite thing. Anyway, our house caught fire, it's the one down at the bottom of the hill, over there," she pointed to a burned-out hulk, next to a crater in the street. "His wife was coming home from work, and was caught by that blast." Jandy became quiet, "None of us saw our parents again either. He saved us... and took us in. We became his family. Shabda was baby-sitting us at the time."

"We've all lost loved ones here." Ashling smiled sweetly, "You'll fit right in. We'll be your family, too." She smiled at Colby.

Nyler thought the boy looked about six-years-old. Colby kept his hand on his Sand Cat's head as they all sat talking. Moonda was a tawny, golden tabby with a dark M on her forehead, eyes as green as jade, not unlike Jandy's. Nyler could see she was a young cat, but full of knowing.

"Come in, come in." Jack encouraged. "You're probably hungry and tired. You'll have to tell us where you've been and how you stayed safe over these last three years."

*****

Nyler liked Adam Shummar, not only was he a healer, a doctor, which they often needed, as Ashling constantly came home with scraps and cuts from her savaging and scouting with Jump, but also because Adam sang. The man and his son, Colby, could sing like creation could be made anew.

He loved to hear them sing. Adam would get everyone involved. Those were the best evenings. Learning songs. Lifting spirits. It was good.

Kadora and Jack were spending a lot of time together. We all watched things develop between them. Jack was forty and Kadora was thirty-five. They both wanted children, but neither had been blessed in that way. Anyway, by natural means, and not only by adoption. It was something we all heard from them, they talked about it often. Nyler didn't think it was going to take long before a mate bonding would proceed, and sleeping arrangements would alter. Maybe two, if Nyler could screw up his courage to ask Shabda.

*****

Mirra was close to giving birth. We were all on edge with anticipation. We all wanted to be there when it happened. No one left home for a couple of days. Finally, it was time.

Mirra had chosen a corner kitchen cupboard, we had filled it with soft blankets, and a puppy liner they could remove once the kittens came. It was warm there next to the oven. They could leave the cupboard doors open. They crowded around, sat on the floor. It wasn't fast... but none of them had anywhere they had to be, Adam sang, they all joined in. It seemed that it soothed Mirra, and eased the births. They all felt a part of it.

The first born was black like Jarin, shorthaired. Such a tiny bit of life, yet it wabbled its way to a teat, hungry already. It is tough work being born. She had four beautiful babies, who all found their way to dinner.

The first black one, then two grey short haired kittens, and a runt that was a light blue grey with long hair. We wouldn't know their names for weeks, and days to tell if they are male or female. Mirra and the other Sand Cats would let us know, when it was time to know.

Nine people and five adult Cats and four kittens. Our Peaceable Community was growing. Contentment lived in our hearts. Not that so many people in one house didn't run into some issues now and then, but we talked out those issues. Misunderstandings were talked through, not ignored, they were talked about till they were understood. In that way, contentment grew, along with compassionate, forgiving Love. Living together for the common good.

FINDING THE LOST LUMDIE
Linda McGeary

# CHAPTER EIGHTEEN

Shortly after the kittens were born, they had their first mate bonding. "Come on Jack, sing the wedding song." Winshaw, acted like a music conductor, waving his hands in swooping motions, "Come on... Here comes the bride... to stand by your side," Everyone joined in as Kadora walked down the length of the room, everyone but Nyler, he didn't know that song. Kadora stopped in front of Jack. The white dress was form fitting, a long veil from the shoulders. She glowed. Her brown eyes met Jacks gray eyes with a dance of merriment. Their smiles were dazzling.

Nothing for her head as they all told Nyler was traditional, but Kadora said she didn't need that, as she had been married before and he died in the bombing, just as Jack's wife had. She'd said she didn't even need a fancy dress, but that was special because Ashling gave it to her.

No one knew how Ashling had found an actual wedding dress, one that was intact, and fit, but one day she came home with it in her backpack and told Jack and Kadora it was time to dress up.

We had all laughed, but that evening, the couple announced the community was "to be their witnesses to a life mate bonding as Nyler called it."

"A wedding." Everyone else called it.

Today they faced each other. Nyler to say the words of joining.

"We gather to witness the visible sign of your love for each other. A life mate bond as true as that of the sun rising, as delicate and delightful as the light of a full moon, as beautiful and sure as the smiles on your faces. We are here to witness the joining of two hearts. Always two, but also one, united by that special love," Nyler couldn't help but glance toward Shabda, as he said this, he saw a wide smile on her face and eyes that shone with promise of their own. He lost track of his thoughts, "United… Uh… united… by that special love… that brings new creation into being." He finished.

"Kiss. Kiss. Kiss." Ashling, Colby, Jandy, and Winshaw shouted and then laughed and clapped with joy when they did.

Colby said, "Oooh, yuck." Which made us all laugh and clap some more.

It was right, and sweet, and solid. Family. There was great joy in our celebrating.

*****

The Sand Kittens were three months old when the Community had an honoring ceremony. All our adult partner Sand Cats had dreamed us the kitten's names. We were all delighted with them. We acknowledged each one and their gift of dreams to us. Love and dreams.

Cedar, first born, black shorthaired like his father, Jarin, Shabda's companion Sand Cat. Forest, second born, he had dark grey shorthair. Mina, she was light grey, shorthaired. And the littlest, Adria, long haired like her mother, Mirra, but the lightest blue grey anyone had ever seen, soft and silky. She was feisty, too, even though she was the smallest. Nyler enjoyed watching them tumble and play. Hide and pounce on each other, with a tiny hiss or yowl, paws raised, batting at each other.

Then they would settle in the birth cupboard in a pile to sleep and dream. Already they were sending out wisps and fragments of dreams to our Community. Clearer every night. Everyone in the community had wispy images of the old cave on the other side of the valley. They all talked about what that could mean. It wasn't an easy distance, with more of the unfriendly-looters in Sea Side these days, it wasn't safe in the middle distance to his old cave. But it was back up if they ever needed it, Jack had said. Nyler hoped they never would, need it, as he'd grown accustomed to the ease and comfort of this new, to him, kind of house, with electricity. Nyler knew they would eventually outgrow this house, it was already tight, because they could only use the bottom half that had no street facing windows. And for some reason, Jack wanted all of them to be together on the same floor, there on that lower level.

Nyler knew he wanted to ask Shabda to marry him. He wanted to have children with her. He dreamt, he knew it would happen, he didn't know what he was waiting for. It's not like they hadn't talked about mate bonding and children. He knew they would love children with their whole souls.

Maybe, it was the fear he found unexpectedly lodged in his chest, like a stone wedged in his throat, choking him. Not all the time, but would appear out of nowhere every now and then. Fear for children raised in this time. This place. But then he remembered he'd had a little brother who had died in a wagon accident... People get old and die. He knew all that. Maybe the truth of it was that all times, all life... was always at the edge. The question was always how do we make the life and time we have the best it can be. The best for everyone. And what about the ones they called looters? The unfriendlies. Could they ever be reached? Would they ever see what it could mean to themselves to be in a Peaceable Community? Could they ever be turned from hate? He himself would have to be careful. For he believed fear was the pathway to hate, and hate burned everything to ash. All you had to do was look at the ruin of Sea Side to know that was true.

*****

A week after the wedding. Ashling was going to what she called downtown. Where what was left of the big stores were. There were so few people left in Sea Side anymore you could still find things useful to the community. It was Ashling and Jump's talent. She was very good at finding. She had just celebrated her tenth birthday, small for that age, they said. Nyler thought the people where bigger than his people from before as a general population.

Ashling was fine boned, and slight, though. She always reminded him of a cousin of his as blood lines went. The Peaceable Communities never paid much attention to that sort of thing, even though they knew their close relatives. All the people were of great worth in any of the communities. They were *all* Kin.

"Hey, Ash," Winshaw trotted up and handed her a list of things that Adam needed for their medicine chest. "This is your new list. Do you want me to come with?"

"No. You make too much noise, Jump and I can hide in smaller places without you around."

"Well, pay attention." Nyler said, "Stay focused. Don't let things distract you. We've seen more signs of the unfriendlies out there close by lately."

Ashling rolled her eyes. "Looters, Ny. Looters."

"Yeah," Winshaw agreed, "Don't go getting full of yourself Ash, just because you're our best scout and finder of things." He, ruffed her hair, and gently punched her shoulder.

"Follow Jumps lead." Nyler patted her shoulder. "Cats have a keener sense of place and what's going on around them, than we do." Ash rolled her eyes again.

"Yeah, I know. And they hear a lot better than people, too."

"You know if he vanishes, you'd better follow." Jandy added. "Don't wait to see if there's any one around, just hide."

"I know. *I know*!" Ashling jogged down the balcony steps to the side yard, and out to the cracked and broken sidewalk. "I've been doing this since I was Colby's age." Nyler could hear her mutter, and shook his head and chuckled. She was always so sure of herself, he thought. She was an amazing kid, and Nyler trusted the White Dragon to keep watch over her out there.

They watched Ashling and Jump head out. An empty backpack on her back to collect up the things on the list. For Nyler the times any of the people went out there, were hard on him, until they returned home, safe and sound, as Jack would say, it was hard to relax, or lose himself in his carvings. He knew to worry was wasted time. But today he felt extra twitchy for some reason.

They had been refilling what Jack called the bomb shelter that was dug into the hillside and connected to the basement of the house, years before the war started. It had a hidden entrance from the kitchen down there where they lived most of the time. Behind the birth cupboard, there was a sliding panel big enough for grownups to go through quickly and easily. The shelter was nearly full of emergency supplies again. Supplies that had been used up over the last three years before Nyler came.

Water, backpacks, flashlights and binoculars (such amazing things) were being replenished now, home packaged dry goods, canned foods they had done, blankets... you name it, if you might need it, Jack had thought of it.

They all said it was because he was a fireman. Nyler understood that to mean Jack had the heart to run into burning buildings to save people he didn't know. That was the bravest thing Nyler had ever heard of a person doing. That he had a mind that thought of things and how they might happen before they happened. It was like he had the spirit of a Sand Cat, even before they would dream something to him, he had thought it. Prepared for it. Most extraordinary. The respect Nyler felt for Jack was deeper than he had felt for anyone else in his life, except his father and mother.

Since Adam, Colby and Kadora joined them, Jack believed the more people they had living there the more likely the unfriendlies were to find them eventually. So, he insisted they refill the shelter as back up. Jack always, said, "A good plan is only as good as your backup plan."

Nyler had never had to live where things were as uncertain as they were here in this place, in this time.

*****

Everyone was gathered in the basement kitchen – Great room space. It was getting dark and Ashling wasn't back yet. They were all on edge.

"She may be pinned down somewhere and can't move without them finding her." Winshaw was pacing. "That happened once before. Remember Jack?"

"Maybe we should go out looking for her," Jandy said, chewing at her fingernails, and making little spitting noises.

"No, we might blunder right into the ones she's avoiding." Jack said, "The ones we don't want to get found by. We stay put. She's a smart kid. She knows what to do."

The Sand Cats began to meow, they formed a tight circle with the kittens in the middle and we got an image of Ashling with blood on her face, a gang of four men and a young woman, dragging Ashling up the balcony steps. Then an image of the shelter and all the cats inside, except Jump.

Colby jumped up and let the cats through the cupboard, into the anti-chamber to the shelter behind the cupboard. He climbed into the cupboard on top of a pile of folded blankets and shut the doors, just as the Cats sent that very image to each of us.

"I've never had a waking dream before." Nyler said, "The Cats are reassuring us to be calm. Trust them! This is a fortune wrapped in a misfortune. Trust the blessing will come, the fortune will unwrap itself."

"I have a back-up plan for this." Jack said, "Don't panic!"

The sharp sound of breaking glass, and splintered wood up-stairs, and angry voices.

"It's not this house!" Ashling shouted, so loud we could all hear it.

A young man and a woman came down the stairs. Guns drawn. "Not the right house, huh?" the young woman said and slapped Ashling across the face, caused her to fall against the railing.

"Don't lie to me." A big burly young man, said. "Don't ever do that again. Or you may not live to regret it."

Ashling broke away from the woman and ran to Jack, who took her under his arm, shielded. Kadora came and wrapped around Ashling on the other side.

"I'm sorry Dad, I tried to lead them away." Even though Ashling loved Jack like a father, she never called him that. It was always, Jack. *Was she trying to reassure Jack? Tell us something?*

"Yes. She did that alright. But one of my boys followed her from a distance." He held up a small hand-held device. "We stay in touch, me and my men."

"I recognize you." Adam said, "I saved your life four years ago. I dug a bullet out of your back. Your name... was... something like," he snapped his fingers, "Danby..."

"*Shut up!* You don't need to know my name to do what I say. Yeah, I can see, *that* was you. You did a good job Doc. One of my battle scars, women love them. But don't count on that givin' you special privileges. Uh, uh."

"We could use a Doctor, Dan." Said the woman, dressed in a heavy coat, twice her size and long baggy pants. Nyler saw anxiety etched in every young line of the woman's face. A face he first thought hard and mean, but was really scared and tense, trying for this Danby fellow's approval.

Nyler watched a kid that looked about the same age as Winshaw, they could have been brothers they look so much alike. The kid was staring at Jack.

"Hey! Aren't you the fireman?" the kid asked from the bottom step of the stairway.

Jack took the kid in, from head to foot. "You've grown. How are your folks?"

"You saved us from our house on fire five years ago." The kid said with awe in his voice. "You remember me?" he stepped down into the room. "My dad died a year later from a heart attack… thank goodness he never had to see any of this." He made a quick glance toward Dan. "But Mom…"

"*Oh, come on!*" Dan shouted, "This isn't a reunion here. I'm giving orders. You all work for me now! Do you understand that? Hey, Doc. Where's your kid, didn't you have a boy? Where is he?"

"He's probably hiding, he was scared when you broke down our door." Adam gave the man, Dan, a direct stare from under hooded eyes, brows pinched together, lips a tight straight line.

"Men," Danby said to the four guys who had followed him down into the kitchen, living room. "Take whatever you want, whatever you find that looks useful. Is that dinner I smell, Emmm. Bring that too." The man gave a hard glare at the young woman with him, "I haven't eaten a decent meal since… Oh, when was it you joined us? You can't cook worth sh…"

Another man with a huge canvas bag and a dog came running down the stairs, interrupting Danby.

Nyler tensed as the dog went around the kitchen sniffing.

"And if I find you're harboring Cats, *you're all dead meat.*" He snarled loudly, "A minute after those damned alien mind controlling fur bags bite it. I *hate* Cats."

His men went around opening drawers and cupboards, searching bedrooms. Filling bags and backpacks. One of them put the dinner in a cardboard box, hot pots and all, and carried it up the stairs. Another man got to the birth cupboard, secret entrance, and jerked the cupboard doors open, Colby screamed so loud, Danby nearly shot his own foot off, the bullet was only inches away from his toes. The sound of the blast was so loud in the enclosed space, the dog yelped and ran up the stairs and outside.

"So, there's the kid," Danby laughed nervously.

"Don't hurt my son." Adam yelled, holding both hands up, and patted the air with his open palms. "Please!"

"We'll take those blankets." Dan glared at them all. "We've got some new men coming in. Load up what you can carry. We'll come back for the women tomorrow. Get your stuff ready, ladies." Dan said to the women. "You're mine now!"

"It's the way he keeps his 'workers' in line." The kid said in a low tone close to Jack, he whispered, "He's got my mother."

"That's right kid. So, you do what I say! Stay here and guard my prizes... My new women. Don't forget..." he laughed, "I've got your dear old mom." Danby's eyes were colder than stone, there was a deadness behind them that gave a jolt to Nyler's spine when their eyes met.

Dan looked around meaningfully, gaze lingering on the women and girls with unclean thoughts, Nyler could see it written all over the man's smirking face.

"I'm taking the brat with me." Dan grabbed Ashling roughly by the shoulder, pulling her away from Jack and Kadora, and pushed her up the stairs. At the top, "Remember Kid, John's up on the roof. He's watching, too. So don't do anything stupid. We'll be back tomorrow to pick up anything we've missed. You thought you had a sweet setup here, Mr. Jack, the fireman." Dan huffed, with lips curled down, the odor of hate about him.

Then he smirked again as he looked down at Shabda, Kadora, and Jandy one last time as he ascended the stairs. The meaning of it made Nyler physically ill and his blood ran cold. It made him realize for the first time a root cause of war. The fear, that overcomes love. Fear that tracks down hate to fortify against loss. But never really fulfills its promise of safety, or getting what you think you want.

When the unfriendlies were outside, Jack said to no one in particular, "Strength whispers. Weakness screams."

# CHAPTER NINETEEN

"So, can you trust me?" Jack asked, "Have you ever had a Dream Cat?"

Nyler held his breath, as he watched the two of them. The young man Danby left behind and Jack, sitting on the edge of the couch, leaning forward, towards each other intently concentrating on their conversation.

"I seem to remember you were pretty broken up about the dog and cat that didn't make it out of the fire when your house burned down."

The kid nodded. "You're right. I had a Cat who dreamed with me." He showed me things, the fire, and I told my dad what I'd dreamt. He said it was just a silly dream, not to worry. I knew it was more than that because I'd had other dreams that came true, but... he was my dad. I thought, didn't he know more than me? I was only ten. But then our house burned down. So, I knew my Cat's dream was true." He lifted his chin, his eyes misted up. "Yes, if you have a Dream Cat and can save my mom, I will believe you, I'll do whatever you say." His mouth twisted, "My Cat, Tink, could have saved herself... But Button was only a puppy, only a year old, and he got trapped in the basement and she wouldn't leave him. Their deaths haunt me."

"What's your name? I can't remember." Jack put his big hand on the young man's shoulder.

"Benjamin."

"Do you mind being called Ben?" Winshaw asked, "My sister, Ash, shortens everyone name if she can. "More efficient, she says. I'm Win. This is Ny, and Shab, and Jack's wife Kadora. Or just Dora. The Doc is Adam and his son is Colby."

"Yeah, Ben is fine. It's what my mom calls me."

"Let's join the Cats!" Jack said. "Bring anything you want to keep that the Looters didn't take."

Nyler found his tools untouched. A sure sign the unfriendlies would rather take than work.

They all retreated to the shelter. Closing the secret panel and a second piece that looked like wall, locking it in place.

"Even if they tear the kitchen apart for some reason, they won't find the anti-chamber to the shelter. And even if they did, they couldn't open the door. They don't have the code." Jack said. "My five brothers and I built this house, and the shelter, because we could see all this coming years before the war… Things just kept getting worse and worse. The hate." he said and he punched in the code to open the door to the shelter.

"You never said you had brothers." Jandy was the first into the storage area. They all followed.

"There were six of you?" Winshaw said amazed. "Why don't we know them? Where are they?"

"What happened to them?" Colby asked, worriedly.

"Dead." Jack's tone was flat, "Like so many in our families." He closed and locked the door. "The war took three of them right off, the other two worked the slaughter house up the valley about twenty miles from here. They disappeared in the dust of war. If they were still alive, they would have come here looking for me." The big man sat on one of the bunks, looked down at his empty, work roughened, hands. I was the oldest brother. I should have gone looking for them sooner than I did… but my wife…" Jack stopped talking and looked up and smiled at Kadora. "Sometimes…"

Kadora sat down next to him and took one of his hands in hers. "I know. I understand. I remember what those early days were like. If it hadn't been for taking care of Colby, and helping Adam, I don't know what might have happened to me."

"Jack, I think you have a plan you haven't shared with us yet." Nyler looked at the man he'd come to regard with great respect and trust in his abilities to plan ahead. "There's more to this shelter than you've told us, I think."

"Yea." He sighed, "Much more. My back up plan. But we all need to sleep if we can. The Cats need to sleep, they need to dream to Ben's mom, and Ashling. Jump is still out there, too. And will find Ash," Jack looked at Ben, "she will get your mom out of the place Dan is keeping them in. That man is no match for the Cats." Then he grinned. "If we can sleep, the Cats will show us what comes next."

Everyone, all nine people, found a bunk and got as comfortable as they could. The Cats, also curled up with them. The littlest kitten curled up with Ben. Nyler felt a click in his mind. Companions. He knew it. Little Adria had chosen her bond person. Ben's hand curled protectively around the small blue gray kitten and pulled her close to his chest. Nyler smiled in spite of their grim circumstances.

They did sleep. And the dreams came. Vivid strong dreams.

*Ashling was shoved into a large basement room of a fancy downtown estate, there was a woman with long scraggly blonde hair, and bruises on her face, the door slammed, it made the woman jump out of her chair. Maybe she was thirty-eitht or so. You could tell the blonde woman, Ben's mother, was upset, because the unfriendlies had taken another young girl.*

*"I'm Ash, You're Maggie." Ash said, "And I've come to rescue you. To get you out of here." She whispered.*

*"What... How did you know my name?"*

*"My Dream Cat is outside and he shows me things in dreams. I know how to get us out. I got caught on purpose so you could join us. I've seen you and your son, Ben, for some time now."*

*"I can't leave, they have Ben."*

*"No, he's with us now. I want you to close your eyes..." Ashling touched Maggie's forehead with the palm of her left hand. "See... the Dream Cats can show us what we need to know. They can dream us a way out of here. And I have a safe place we can go."*

*"Oh!" Maggie exclaimed. "I saw Ben... sleeping on a bunk... with others there, too. Just a flash. How did you do that? It will make Dan furious." Maggie paced the floor. "But if Ben is safe, I'll try anything to get away from that man. Ben used to have a Cat who could dream with him. He told me his cat showed him the fire, before it burned our house down. So how does that work? How do we do this?"*

*"Tomorrow, they will leave to go back to Jack's house, we will have a good two hours to get away. Dan will only find the guard left behind at Jack's house. The one on the roof. He will have a hard time explaining how nine people left the house, just vanished, without being seen. But I've already dreamt that part. I just wasn't supposed to talk about it yet. Jack has a secret way out no one else knows about, yet. Jump showed me."* Ashling pulled a bottle of pills out of her pocket. *"And, so do we. This'll put the two watching us to sleep. I picked it up when I knew we would need it for tomorrow morning. Then we take water and food and go to Nyler and Jubilee's cave on the north west side of town. They won't know where we've gone... Well, Nyler and the others will, but not Dan. Not even that worthless dog of his will be able to track us. My cat Jump knows the way."*

*"You're sure this will work?"*

*Ashling smiled, "Without a doubt."*

*****

When they all woke up Jack showed them the door in the back of the shelter behind some shelving. Another thick door like the coded one they came through from the house the night before.

"This was an old mine decades ago. Actually, my great grandfather used to work in this mine. The refinery was about twenty miles away. Down the valley. Down this track. When the mine played out, everyone in my family pooled their money and bought the mine and refinery building and turned it into a slaughter house. Which we worked till the war came. Except me, I became a fireman early on, a long time before we bought the property, I'd rather save people than kill them. My three brothers just younger than me, joined the army. We were informed when they were killed in a troop transport plane crash."

Jack heaved on the heavy door, "Help me with this!" Jack groaned, the heavy door screeched, Nyler pushed with him to open it and there was a long tunnel stretching into the dark.

"It hasn't been opened in a couple of years. That was the last time I checked the tracks and the car. The slaughter house, firming up my back up plan."

He flipped a switch, just like Ashling had done that first day for Nyler, showing what electricity was, and light shot down the length of the dark tunnel. "I hooked it up to the solar power, back when my brothers and I planned this as a secret exit if we ever needed it."

"This is so *cool*." Winshaw said, "Why didn't you tell us this was here?"

"Because it was a secret. Secrets kept, can't be told." Jack answered. "This is our way to Nyler's cave on the other side of the valley." Jack gave Nyler a look. "Isn't that right? Hasn't Jubilee and the other Dream Cats been showing us your cave for weeks now?"

Jack looked at Ben, "Your mom, Ashling and Jump will be there before us, if what we just all dreamt is true. And I have no reason to doubt it is. We need to get a move on. Load this rail car with everything from the storage room. Even the thin mattresses off the bunks."

It took them a few hours of work, many trips to load the mine car which sat on the tracks.

"How does it move." Ben asked, Nyler had wondered that too.

"It's electric." Jack said, "The Cats can ride, but we're going to have to walk."

"Twenty miles," Nyler figured in his head. "I'm not sure what time it is right now, but we will most likely have to sleep in this tunnel tonight, and keep going to where ever the end of this track takes us in the morning."

"You're right!" Jack laughed, "Kadora, did you put the food and blankets on top?"

"Yes, just like Forest showed me, even before I understood what I was doing it for." She gave the kitten a scratch under his chin, he lifted his head staring up at her, blinked in Cat adoration. "Good boy, smart kitty." He exposed his neck, in pure pleasure, he loved the attention, loved Kadora. Nyler smiled, another bond.

*****

They walked in the dim light, tired, and hungry by the time they came to a niche in the wall that was an obvious resting station. An old rickety, rough wooden table, some squeaky chairs and five wire frame beds, with no mattresses. They ate, and curled up as best they could, where ever they could. The youngest ones on the stone floor with blankets and pillows, snuggled close together for warmth. Nyler was on the floor with the kids. The Sand Cats already nestled with the person of their choice. There was little talking. After eating, they wanted sleep more than anything. Hope filled them as they thought of tomorrow and the way ahead.

*****

*Dan and his crew came up the balcony steps. He waved to the man on the roof. The man waved back. "I'm coming down. I'll meet you inside."*

*The dog sniffed and pawed around a flowerbed the Cats sometimes used as their bathroom, it got excited and howled wildly. Dan kicked it. "Get away from there. You stupid animal."*

*The young woman with Dan, called the dog to her. It was obvious she didn't like the way Dan treated the dog, any more than the way he treated her. It was also clear she was pregnant. She held a hand protectively over her rounded stomach. She wasn't wearing a coat today like she had the day before. The reason for her anxiety and the need of a doctor was now obvious.*

*They all go inside and find the house empty. "What the hell? Where are they?" Dan yelled as the guard came down the stairs.*

***"Where are they?"** He screamed and grabbed the front of the smaller man's coat, jerked him off the ground, tossed him against a wall. "Don't tell me you just let them walk out of here without noticing? Did you fall asleep? Again?"*

*The man stood, held up his hands, "No!" eyes wide. "Hey man, nothing like that happened. I would have heard them, seen them, I took something to stay awake. I didn't fall asleep! They couldn't get out... couldn't. Not..."*

*Dan was working himself into a full-blown rage, he started smashing things. He threw anything not nailed down. Dishes and vases, sweeping pictures off the walls, but none of it seemed to satisfy his wrath, only fed it. He drew his gun and shot his night watchman between the eyes, the dead man thumped to the floor. Eyes wide open with a dead glassy stare. Blood welled up and pooled in the dead man's eye and dripped to the floor. The dog started whining, Dan shot the animal, too. The woman dropped to the floor and crawled behind a couch whimpering like the dog had done just seconds before. Dan emptied his gun into the walls, only barely refraining from killing anymore of his men.*

*"That damned kid was supposed to be watching them inside." Dan screamed. "I'll kill his mother, and that fucking brat."*

*He tore out of there like a missile, leaving the pregnant woman behind cowered on the floor with the bloody bodies of the man and dog, in the shot up, shattered house that now smelled of iron red hot cordite, and befoulment.*

*The men with Dan could barely keep up, he was on such a tear. By the time he got to their base compound an hour away, and slammed into the room where Ashling and Maggie were kept, he discovered his two guards asleep in their chairs, leaning on the table. He would have shot them too, but his gun was still empty, it just clicked and clicked as he pulled the trigger, rage screaming. He threw it against the wall, picked up a bat and started beating the two sleeping men.*

*The men who followed him scattered back out the door. It was too much, they had had enough of Dan's unpredictable rages, his mean, hateful, murderous actions.*

*They wouldn't be back. Dan was his own captive, prisoner to his rages, a boss without a crew.  A man alone... to fester with hate... at least for now.*

# CHAPTER TWENTY

As Nyler woke, then one by one the others, a silence came with waking. There was no easy chit chat, no idle breakfast talk. They avoided even looking at each other. The dream was still too vivid, heavy on their hearts. As they were leaving to walk the last bit to the slaughter house, an apt place to be going after they had seen what Dan had done. The Cats had kept Colby from seeing any of that. Though the boy knew something bad had happened, he didn't need to have any of those images in his head. The Cats were wise and caring.

Ben broke down crying. "I'm so relived Mom and Ash got out, but that dog wasn't a bad animal. He was actually kind of sweet." He drew his sleeve across his eyes. "Those men didn't deserve to die like that either. They were just too weak to stand up to the bullying and belittling Dan always treated them to. All of us."

"I know." Jack put an arm around the kid and so did Winshaw and Jandy, comforting their new friend, a boy who could be a brother to them.

"That's human nature when something you think is under your control slips away from you." Adam said.

"No!" Nyler shook his head, "That's not human nature, that is human fear. Don't blame that on nature. At some point in his life that was a choice. He may have felt like he had no choice, but there is always a choice. And I can assure you it wasn't the first time he chose to kill. I hope the men who scattered will find a better way to live. A kinder choice to live by.

It didn't take them long to reach the end of the tracks and a wall with a shelter thick door with a code. Once that was opened and they were inside the slaughter house. They couldn't wait to get outside where they could take deep, clean breaths of air.

Jack was laughing so hard, he collapsed on the ground clutching his sides. "Oh, you should have seen your faces."

"*What was that smell*?" Winshaw couched. Spat, and couched some more. Even the Cats seemed overcome by the nasty odors being capable of smelling better than humans. *And Nyler was sure the Cats had known what was coming.*

Half of the people were on the ground, spitting and pulling deep breaths of air into their lungs.

"That was our last plan to keep people out of there, away from my back door." Jack sat up, still chuckling. "We laced the place with enough foul stuff to keep people out of there for a long, long time. Then closed the place up tight just before the war broke out and hoped against hope that it wouldn't be bombed."

"Well," Adam said, "it certainly must have been effective. No one came knocking."

"Even the bombs didn't want to come here." Colby said, and spit.

"Uh, folks," Nyler interrupted, "You realize we have to go back in there, don't you?"

That sobered Jack up, "I'm prepared for that." He got up, put a hanky over his nose and mouth went in by himself. Came out a little later driving a large work crew cab truck with an extra-long bed. The truck stank, too, but would air out... eventually.

"Don't worry," Jack said, "The lock box is air tight." He unlocked it and handed six gas masks out to as many as were willing to go to work, loading up the truck bed.

"When you six get tired, we can switch out, until we get it all stowed." Jack said, "We'll leave the truck out here with open doors to air out." Then he showed them how the gas masks worked, and they went to it. And it really wasn't too bad.

They shared the responsibility and had the mine car goods loaded into the bed of the truck in much less time than it had taken the day before, to load the mine car than it did to load the bed of the truck, and tie it down with a tarp, and the people climbed in the crew cab and Jack drove through the valley, to the hills and mountains on the other side.

It took more than three hours to get across because of all the back tracking they had to do. The road conditions were bad, blocked, or the streets cratered.

Nyler clung on to the handle bar above the door. "I've never been in anything like this metal beast-less wagon. It is quite scary how it bumps and jerks. The speed." He said as the truck juddered over broken concrete, and he clutched even tighter to the handle thinking of his brother and the horse drawn wagon accident that killed him.

Kadora sat between Jack and Nyler on pillows and blankets. Three were on a fold down bench seat behind the front seats. And three on the back bench seat were knocking knees with those opposite them, creating a bit of comic relief. It was tight with all the Cats there too, but it was a big truck meant to carry a big crew.

*****

Hours later, they pulled into a neighborhood much like Jack's only on the other side of the valley but still miles away from the cave and ocean.

"I think... We're just about as close as we're gonna get in this rig." Jack said. "It'll probably take a few hours more to get to your cave on foot, Nyler, we're quite a way down the valley from the ocean at this point. But there's a road that goes along the other side of this ridge. I don't think it is drivable though. That side of the cliffs took quite a beating in the war. Maybe we can find a way closer... but not tonight... not in the dark."

"But what about our supplies?" Jandy worried. "We can't make that trip even in the light with all this stuff."

"I know." Jack answered. "We need a good night's sleep so we can check in the light of day to see what's what tomorrow. I'm pretty sure, all of these houses on the ridge are empty. When the bombs began to drop, people fled, I never heard of anyone coming back. Obviously not all of them were bombed, burned or destroyed... but the people moved south, down the valley, anyway, where it was said there was less destruction and fighting going on. One of these houses should be secure enough for us to sleep in. Maybe we can park the truck behind a house to keep it out of sight… Just in case there are 'Unfriendlies' lurking around." Jack said giving Nyler a glance as if to say, OK, I'm using your term for looters.

"If we can't get the truck closer, we can jury rig a wagon of some sort or a travoy to pull the stuff with us tomorrow." Said Winshaw, "Then we won't have to carry it all." He shrugged, "And we won't have to make as many trips back to retrieve it."

They piled out of the truck looking for the best house to crash in.

"Sounds good to me." Jack chuckled, kissed the top of Kadora's head. "Sounds good."

"A good long sleep sounds good to me," Kadora yawned, and wrapped her arms around Jack, and put her head on his chest almost asleep on her feet.


*The Cats led the way. A circuitous route across the ridge line of cliffs that had been fine huge fancy houses at one time not too far in the past. The Cats walked before them, they all followed on foot, while Jack drove the truck around broken roads, and bombed and burn out houses. Some houses stood unharmed with empty holes, or burned-out shells of houses twenty feet away next door. So random. In this manner they came within a mile or so of Nyler's cave. They hid the truck in a stand of teakwood trees. They had found a couple of wheelbarrows, and a large motor cycle wagon they loaded on the truck from the house they spent the night at, they filled them up with goods from the truck bed and followed the Cats around the brow of the hill to the outside edge of the cliffs overlooking the bay.*

*Nyler grinned to himself even in his sleep. There was Ashling and Ben's mother, Maggie, waiting for them.*


The next morning, they followed the lead of the adult Cats, while the people shared the burden and pleasure of carrying the kittens. Shabda and Nyler walked side by side. The kitten, Cedar, the one who looked the most like her Cat, Jarin, he cuddled under her coat, in an inside pocket, purring loudly, asleep.

After a long arduous day on foot, with Jack driving the truck they came to the teakwood grove.

They all sighed and stretched with relief, knowing they were very close. They rested and ate. Talked about what and how to distribute the goods and the best way to get them to the cave.

"Once we're in Nyler's cave we can relax for a time. Reassess what to do next." Jack said, "We will have to make another trip. We won't be able to carry all this in two wheelbarrows and a wagon… even with each of us carrying what we can in our backpacks."

"But we are close." Nyler noticed the Cats, even the kittens had disappeared from their company. "The Cats have gone on ahead."

Jack and Kadora smiled at each other, "They are letting Ashling and Maggie know we're on our way." Kadora said, patting Ben's knee as he sat closest to her and Jack on the ground, to rest and eat.

"I can't wait to see my mother." Ben grinned. "This nightmare is finally over. I was always afraid to leave her for fear someone would hurt her. She was always afraid I wouldn't come back."

"We will be safe now." Jandy's eyes grew misty, "I can feel it. We are safe here."

"Did any of you see what Moonda dreamt to me?" Colby asked shyly, "There are others coming. We will need a bigger cave."

"Well, that's a problem for another day." Nyler smiled at Colby and put an arm around the boy. They were sitting on a log together eating apples.

"Did you know there is a White Dragon guarding our caves front door?" Colby asked looking up at Nyler. "Moonda showed me. She also showed me that we should make a back door, too."

"I will tell you a story about that White Dragon when we are all settled into the cave, when our work is done." Nyler said. "I know I've told you some of the history, but I'll tell you more stories of the Peaceable Communities. As close as I know the history myself, from the Sand Cats… uh… Dream Cats dreams to me about the original Lumdie. About the Kin."

"But for now, it's time for us to move out, while we still have daylight." Adam said. "He loves stories, that kid. He'll keep you telling him every exciting thing that's ever happened to you, Nyler."

They all chuckled. "But I want to hear too," Jandy said, Winshaw and Ben, seconded that. "I know Ashling will want to hear your stories."

"Up and at em'." Jack commanded, a content expression on his face. Heartsease… visible, thought Nyler.

Linda McGeary

# CHAPTER TWENTY-ONE

"Ash," Winshaw and Jandy ran to hug Ashling. "Oh, when they took you away with them, we were so scared for you." Jandy cried, and hugged so tight she nearly squeezed the life out of Ashling. "We should have known. You're like Jack. You always have a back-up plan."

"We're so glad you were able to get out." Winshaw beamed happily at his sister and Maggie. "Both of you."

Ben and his mother, clung to each other. Tears mingled with grateful relief.

After everyone greeted Maggie, and loads redistributed to share the burden before they headed around the brow of the cliff face and into Nyler's cave.

"Oh! Look!" Shabda pointed. The sun spilled vermillion across a low bank of clouds. "The sunset has turned to sea crimson." Nyler came up behind her, encircled her in his arms, she leaned against him, "It's so beautiful from up here." She breathed in a deep breath of sea air. So did Nyler. "It was always one of the things I loved best about this place. Watching the sun go down."

"Did you know he knew our names before he ever met us?" Ashling grabbed Shabda's arm. "Come here, let me show you."

"Ash," Shabda pulled away, "what are you... right now I just want to see the sunset."

"No. Come see this, all of you."

The nine, now eleven, crowded into the cave, Jack had a very tight squeeze but was finely in, the fire warmed and lit the place. Ashling shined her flashlight on the white stone by the narrow doorway, showing them all. "You'll have to add more names, Ny. Lots more names." And she grinned.

"We cleaned it up, and swept the place out in preparation for all of you. Jump showed us in a dream last night when you were coming." Maggie smiled. "It is such a relief to be here with family." She hugged Ben again. "Even a bare cave is a better place to live with good people, than with those hateful people in a fine house. I will have to get used to the idea of dreaming with Cats though, that has been outside my experience before now," said Maggie.

*****

Everyone was gathered around the fire. Nyler noticed that Ashling and Maggie had found rocks and ringed the fire. The sleeping mats, pillows, blankets had been arranged close to the fire, but with the large rocks around the fire so no one would roll into the flames in their sleep. Nyler had made sure the stone was the kind that could withstand the heat.

"You did well, Ashling, some rock will explode if over-heated." Nyler said. "How did *you* know that?"

"School." She shrugged. "Back when we were going. A forest ranger showed us a film about camping. And I remembered he said don't use porous rock for lining a firepit." A one shoulder, shrug this time, "And Jump showed me where to find the right kind." She looked at Nyler and grinned.

He laughed. "Of course. The Cats can help us with a lot of what we need."

They had all gathered around the fire to eat the evening meal, sitting on their sleeping mats. It was their first night in the cave.

"But… we have to do some of what Jack calls brain storming, for most of it." Nyler looked around the circle of people. "Working together is what makes a Peaceable Community. We talk until things are obvious. We listen until things are clear. We try different things until something works. We learn as much from what doesn't work as what does."

"Like privacy." Jack said looking over at Kadora. "How are we going to do any rooms or niches for our beds and how do we get them off the ground. All of us are ok with roughing it, for now. But what about older people, the people who are coming? There will eventually be older people here. It's not easy for them to get up off the floor."

"Maybe the first thing in order is to find bigger, better tools for stone work." Adam said. "Tools to match the work needed to be done."

"Yeah," Winshaw still eating, mouth full, noisily chewing. "Nyler's tools aren't going to cut all this stone."

"Even if they could," Nyler agreed, "We need to do an examination of the stone itself. We have to know, how deep it goes, how high, where the dirt begins and the stone ends."

"I think I can help with that." Adam joined in. "One of the places, Kadora, Colby and I stayed for a while on our way inland up the valley, was a university campus. It's about a hundred miles from here. They had a storeroom full of odd equipment. Some of them were GPR for the archeology classes, if any of it is still there. Not sure why anyone would want it in the normal course of events, but these days you never know."

"What is GPR?" Nyler asked with a puzzled expression on his face.

"Ground Penetrating Radar." Kadora said, "It can show us, the what and where, of the ground formation around here. Above and below us."

"If they're still there." Jack said. "Maybe there's other things there we could use, even if the GPR machines are gone. Such as wiring this place up for electricity. Maybe we could find a generator and some solar panels, too."

"And if we are all going to help, we would knock this place out a lot faster if we had jack-hammers." Winshaw bumped elbows with Ben. "That would be cool."

Ben held up his hands as if he were holding some kind of handle bar, "Raaata ta ta ta." Making jerking motions. The boys laughed, "Yeah, way cool." They said in unison, and then laughed again slapping hands together. Some strange teenage boy ritual of this time, Nyler guessed.

"I have no idea what a Jack... hammer... is." Nyler appealed with his eyes on Jack. "Do you?"

"Oh yeah! And it could work..." Jack said thoughtfully, "If we could find one, or more. And a generator to go along with them, until we get some power into the caves it will all be by hand, I'm afraid. One of the first things, though, is widening the doorway a bit." His smile became a sleepy relaxed yawn. "It's a bit tight for a fireman I know."

"Maybe we need to take a trip to this university you sheltered in for a while Adam." Shabda said, she sat on the mat next to Nyler, her food bowl in the hammock of her lap, a hand on Nyler's knee.

They ate in silence for a time. Spoons scraping empty bowls. The pot near the fire empty as well. The soup that smelled of greens, onion and potato was gone. It needed salt, but was filling, and delicious none the less, after a day of hard work.

*****

The next day from their vantage point up here Nyler had seen the true extent of the damage the war had caused to the city below. They had worked all day to transfer more things from the truck. Now gathered around the fire for dinner, he wondered aloud.

"What started the war?" Nyler ask, looking around the circle. There was an uneasy movement, a soft shifting about, "I've never asked before, but I'd like to know."

"So, would we." Ben agreed.

"Well," Adam glanced at the people gathered around the fire, faces lit by dancing flame light. Ashling placed another piece of wood on the fire and sparks flew up to the stone ceiling.

"Well." Adam said again, "It started back in the time before time. At the beginning of time, you might say. At first the historians thought it was about survival. Maybe fear that if your tribe shared resources with another tribe there might not be enough for both. In the end it was that and the differences..." He held up his dark bear arm, "skin color, all our different shades. The way people worshiped, or didn't, who you worshiped, the names you used, and the stories that were told about how we all got here. The greed of the rich, the lust of the powerful, revenge for offences done. The anger of the poor... the disenfranchised... the desire for justice." He shrugged. "You name it, and people fought over it. Still are by most accounts. And with every advancement in technology came bigger, and more powerful weapons to kill the *enemy* with... More of the enemy."

"Whoever anyone thought was the enemy." Jack sighed. "It was a mess. Millions and millions of people died on all sides. *And for what? No one won.* Things were destroyed, people killed, and for what? It made no sense to me then or now. In the time before… even families could become enemies and quit speaking to each other." He shook his head, "Those were very dark, sad times."

"And got worse." Adam said, "Everything fell apart. It was the war of words before the war of weapons. A time of *'I have my opinion, and I'm right, therefore you must be stupid or evil, and I can kill you if you disagree with me.'* And they did."

Everyone was quiet for a time, absorbing the peace that gathered around them in that moment, in their humble surroundings, in that softly lite safe environment of kin and cave.

The Cats gathered next to their people, purring a lullaby.

"I think," Nyler stroked Jubilee's fur, and looked around the group, "It's time to heal the wounded. And put the broken back together again."

"Let's sleep on all this for tonight." Kadora said, "I'm sure our direction will be clearer in the morning."

"And we still have the last bit of what we left in the truck to bring in." Ben said, and flopped down, and rolled into his blankets for the night.

"What I'm going to miss," Jandy sighed, "Is a shower, and running water, and…" she looked around and whispered, "A bathroom."

"Oh, of course," Nyler jumped up, "Let me show you the outside privy I bult when I lived here." Then he paused, "Well… the pit should still be there. I doubt the small hut will be… but…"

"I can show her," Ashling hopped up, "Come on Jandy. I know where it is."

$$***** $$

After the rest of the food and remaining things were transferred to the very back of the cave and stacked for future use, and the beds re-arranged, they built a new outhouse over the re-dug pit. "We need to find some lime for this." Jack said, Adam agreed.

Second night, plans formed, people settled on jobs they would do for the coming week.

The next day Jack and Adam packed up for a long scavenger hunt. None of us knew when they'd be back. They headed for the university to look for useful things for the community. The way was rutted, and rubbled, but they had Adam's Sand Cat, Simi, to send back images to the community. They made it around all the debris, pitfalls, and delays, to come to the campus after two days travel. What only took a little more than an hour in the before war times, was now a difficult journey. Including finding enough gas to keep the truck going.

It was exciting to get updated through dreams. We all kept busy. Colby found a nice little bit of ground for a garden, and all the young people were planting the seeds Jack had stored for the three years since the war. Ashling in her exploring found a spring and small pool, and brook, so we had fresh, clean water within carrying distance. Shabda, Kadora and Maggie found an iron grill rack in the stuff from the truck and positioned it on the rocks over the fire for cooking and heating water, for what they called, 'Bird Baths'.

Nyler didn't understand, even after all these months living with them, why a little honest sweat was a problem, but he'd do the 'Bird Bath' too, like everybody else. He wanted to please Shabda. The Peaceable Communities had bathhouses, he remembered that, but in his travels, he had gotten used to a little body odor. Through most of the lands he had traveled over that year, few of the people he met, bathed. But he had to admit when he thought about the bathhouses of his childhood, it was a pleasure to soak in a hot bath.

Shabda and Nyler had set a day for their bonding celebration, for as soon as Jack and Adam got back, for the first mate bonding, 'wedding,' in the caves. He knew the women were making plans. He let them. He just was happy they were happy and doing the preparations. He wouldn't have known what to do.

He was outside with Ben and Winshaw. Watched the sea and sky while the women were all inside… bathing. Ashling was off exploring their hillside and cliff area to the west. You couldn't keep that child from exploring. She wanted to know every foot of land all around the hills and cliffs.

"Oh, there's Ash…" Ben pointed. "She looks excited."

Ashling came over the brow of the west side of the cliff area, toward where the teakwood forest grows further down the ridge where they keep the truck parked when it's here.

"You won't believe what I've found!" Her eyes were shinning, some discovered joy was spilling out of them.

"What?" we all three said at once.

"You have to come see it to believe it." She motioned them to follow her, "Come!"

Nyler hesitated, looked back at the cave entrance, then followed the excited Ashling, her brother Winshaw and Ben.

This path was worse than the old path had been back in the day when he had first come to the cave. But the girl was intrepid. She and Jump had found a way down half way to the ocean. The breakers here were loudly crashing against the cliffs below. A sheer drop of a couple of hundred feet to a rocky shore line. They clung to scrub trees in places where the trail narrowed dangerously.

She stopped in front of an opening in the cliff face. "Oh, I wish I'd had you bring more flash lights." Ashling said. "But I didn't think of it."

"I think your eyes are so bright, you can light the way." Nyler chuckled. "Go on. Show us your discovery."

Ashling led them into a narrow tunnel that descended into the earth on a gentle slope. It was tall enough that Nyler didn't have to bend over except in a few places, but steep enough in one spot they had to brace themselves with arms stretched out, touching the walls of the passageway. They walked by Ashling's flashlight beam, until the space opened up to a huge cavernous space. Big enough to fit maybe hundreds of people. Then Nyler saw the floor in the beam of Ashling's light. It was black and as smooth as glass. It looked like water. She ran out on it, shown the light all around. It was dry rock. Black marble. Images of Heartsease that Jubilee had shown him in dreams about the history of the Peaceable Communities.

"Heartsease!" Nyler breathed in awe.

Was this a new Heartsease? Mother Terra's womb for new birth? A gift of quiet, silent praise, from their Mother to the new Community?

"Heartsease!" Nyler whispered again, "A new place of healing."

# CHAPTER TWENTY-TWO

Except for Simi, Adam's Sand Cat, the other Cats were with Nyler and Kin. The kittens played and grew stronger in body and dream spirit. They received nightly updates from Simi about the progress of Jack and Adam.

At the evening meal, Ben was quieter than usual. He finely spoke, "Even though we don't have cell phones any more, we really don't need em. The Cats show us what we need to know. They communicate with us."

"Jump led me to the... what did you call it?" Ashling said.

"Heartsease." Nyler sat down his bowl. "I know I said I'd tell you about the history of the White Dragon. And Heartsease. Even though Jack and Adam aren't here, we are, and the Cats can dream it to them. Nyler chuckled, "Come on gather in. I'll tell you what I know, what the Sand Cats have shown me of our peaceful beginnings."

"Mother Terra has always been plagued with the choices of savage humanity, just like Adam said about how this last war started. Some people have called this human nature, but that is only half the truth. We do have a nature toward self-preservation, and selfishness, but also self-sacrifice, and selflessness. Humanity, and all things, were created out of a Big Love. We can choose to feed either side of our nature. Loving or fearful. Love is a choice. Hate is a choice. Hate leads to the ruins you see down in Sea Side." Nyler looked at each person present, wishing to pierce their hearts with this knowing.

"When we *know* we are loved..." Nyler paused, and started again "Fear feeds hate, when we cast out fear, when we *know* we are loved. Fear can't exist where love is strong, *known* to be without exceptions. But humanity is also weak and easily fooled into feeding hate, thinking it is the right path, the best way of protection. So, there are wars, and killing. Just like Adam said."

"So, how do we know this Big Love." Colby squinted his eyes at his Cat, Moonda, in the love langue of the Cats. "I know I love Moonda, and she loves me. I know my father loves me. I knew my mother loved me. Even when they scolded me for something I shouldn't have done, I *knew* they loved me. And I *knew* that nothing would ever change that. Even when I was just a baby, really." He thumped a small dark fist against his chest. "I knew that here." He said, "and here," he patted his head. "Are you talking about that kind of knowing?"

Nyler's eyes misted up, he swallowed a lump in his throat, "Yes, Colby, that is exactly the kind of knowing I'm talking about."

"How do we get that kind of knowing." Jandy asked. "If we don't already, have it?"

"Heartsease." Nyler answered. "From what I've seen, and understand, silent listening is the way. Heartsease comforts and discomforts people. The black marble floor of the original Heartsease could reflect what was on the inside of hearts and minds, to help them come to that knowing. That Spirit of Love for all created. The silence taught them, and can teach us how to shed our less than loving actions. The question is always, If I loved that person, what would my behavior toward them look like? What would it feel like? How would it be lived out by actions?"

"There was a Mother Protector, and a Father Protector. They lived in a place called Aggadae. In the creases of the mountain range. When they arrive in the mountains, Heartsease was already there. Then the Lumdie people came, they were also peaceful and lived next to the Harapo Lake and River. The Lumdie built a beautiful city, with fine, rich things. They became the nexus of a trade route. Caravans with trade goods passed by there, life was good. But then 'unfriendly' *Looters*," Nyler nodded toward Ashling, "Marauders, murders, came among the Lumdie, stealing, causing trouble. The Lumdie had no skill for war, didn't want it. They were extraordinary builders. A small band of people came and set up a tent city on the south side of the river, the NiVar, they were skilled in fighting. And for a while they protected the Lumdie from the people who would have taken over. Until a time when greed overcame the NiVar leader and he and his men sacked the city of Harapo. They cast out, or killed, the Lumdie people. The Protectors of Heartsease helped thousands of them escape by means of a stone path through the Aggadae Mountains to the desert beyond. The Father Protector led them to a safe place with a staff and a tabard, and a Sand Cat named Claw."

"What's a tabard?" Colby asked.

"Yeah, I don't know that word either," said Jandy. "And I love words."

"Like a cloak, or sleeveless coat." Nyler cocked his head to one side, "Sort of like your dad's leather duster, Colby, only without sleeves. It was white, made from a Dragon who sacrificed his life to save the Aggadae people once. Well, to save all people, really. Anyone who is willing to be sheltered beneath its wings. Accept the Big Love, and its protection."

"Like us! I've seen it, you know." Colby grinned. "He's here, just outside our entrance. I see him all the time!"

"A dragon?" Ashling scoffed. "A real dragon? Like with fire and everything."

"Aren't dragons supposed to guard treasure, or something?" Winshaw asked.

"And the White Dragon does guard treasure." Nyler agreed, "Us!"

"If there is a White Dragon outside our door, why can't we all see it." Maggie asked skeptically.

Nyler shook his head, "The Dragon shows itself to whomever the Dragon wills to see it. The Dragon has made Colby our witness. He is an honest child. Truth-telling is the highest virtue there is. No community can survive long without it. You can believe the White Dragon is real and really there."

"Nyler," Colby's face shown with solemnity. "The Dragon isn't only White... he is all colors. He is the color of love."

"I didn't know that," Nyler leaned over and put his hand and Colby's shoulder, "Thank you for telling us that. I've only seen it in dreams. Mine and other people's dreams, like a white cloud in the sky, over the desert, like the blessing of promised rain to dry ground. You have seen it with the inward eye, as well as true vision, and with the heart, and that is a great blessing. And I imagine the Dragon can change appearance every second if it wanted to. You are blessed to be able to recognize it in all of its colors."

"So, what happened to the Lumdie who escaped?" Shabda asked, bringing them back to the story. "And what happed to the Aggadae who stayed behind?"

"The NiVar made Kings, a succession of them, King Trabot NiVar the first, down three hundred years, to the seventh King of the same name. The seventh was as full of greed as the first had been, wanting the treasure of Heartsease. Not understanding the treasure *was* Heartsease, and the people themselves." Sighing Nyler looked at his family, his people, "But as here, war came to break their peace. Only four souls escaped from that war. Avril, Zada Zan and one of the king's sons, Baz. And a Sand Cat, named Jag."

"How did they get away?" Kadora placed a log on the fire, it snapped and crackled, lifting the level of light around the tight little group to flicker on faces and ceiling, piercing the shadowy niches of stone, lighting the listening circle.

"The Mother Protector sent her daughter, Zada Zan, and her Cat, Jag, through the Aggadae Mountains on the Stone Path. They both had white hair with a deep purple crown and light lavender at the tips. Anyone who took an oath to protect the peace of Heartsease, their hair would change to this color, man, or woman. Zada Zan was born with hair this color… But she had not vowed being only a baby. After going through the mountain, Zada came to the Red Desert. The staff, guided her, and grew food for them. The tabard, sheltered them, Zada and Jag, it could keep them cool in the heat, and warm in the cold nights.

The tabard, the cloak, was made of the White Dragon's skin.  There were two cloaks, and two staffs. One representing men, one representing women. When Zada and Jag got to the Lumdie on the other side of the desert and they showed her where they had buried her Great, great, great grandfather, when he died, who had led them with his Staff from the Aggadae Mountains to a safe place to live."

"Like here." Colby interjected.

"Yes. Like here. They were the continuance of the Peaceable Community. It was called Stone Haven. The tree at the heart of the place, where they buried Zada's Grandfather, they call it the Grandfather Tree. Zada gave up her Staff to join her Grandfather's staff to become part of Grandfather Tree. And her Tabard. That was the first time the people began to see the Spirit of the White Dragon again, riding the winds above their homes."

"And now, he is with us again." Ben mused.

"Not again," Nyler smiled at Ben. "He never left the Peaceable Communities... Or the world. The Protecting Spirit of... the Dragon of many colors, all colors." He squeezed Colby shoulder, "Has always been with Mother Terra, and all people, will always be with you. No matter in life or death, if we choose, to shelter beneath the wings we will be protected. We will learn more in the listening silence of the cave Ashling found. I believe that is our Heartsease. Our new birthplace as individuals and as a family. A place of trust, blessing, hope, and truth. A new beginning for our Peaceable Community."

*****

Jack and Adam were gone for almost a month. They were on their way home, finally. While they were gone, things had progressed in the cave. They had chipped away at two bed niches, one for Jack and Kadora, and one for Nyler and Shabda, for after the wedding. Nyler had worked hard with what tools he had and what the kids could scavenge in a few houses close enough to the cave. Also, they worked on the place in the long entrance tunnel to the new Heartsease, that needed steps and hand holds to make it safer to enter or exit.

Winshaw and Ben had chopped down a few of the teakwood trees near where Jack had parked the truck before.

"This way Jack can pull in closer to the cave to unload." Ashling explained to Nyler and Shabda, as the guys worked. "And we can use the wood for the firepit."

"Teak is a great wood to carve. These trees here have a beautiful deep mahogany color grain, with a scent that is a little bit spicey and sweet." Nyler said, "But it really isn't good for burning. It takes a long time to ignite, and it burns too hot once going. Though I'm sure we can use it in other ways. We need tables and benches for the common kitchen area."

"It will be great to be able to get closer to the cave," Shabda said and nodded, and smiled at Ashling. "You are right about that."

That night the Cats dreamed with them that Jack and Adam would be home the next day, everyone woke up and set about preparing for a celebration.

"I want to go wait for my Dad." Colby jumped up and down with excitement.

"We can go with him," Ben and Winshaw said, "Make sure he's safe."

The three headed out and the rest of them got a meal going and a blanket attached to two knobs of stone above Jack and Kadora's bed niche, giving them some privacy for his joyous return.

"How soon will ours be finished." Whispered Shabda, in Nyler's ear. Kissing his cheek, hugging him.

He took her in his arms, smiled down at her. "Maybe a day or two." He laughed. "That is if we don't get side tracked, with everything they are bringing in."

"Did I tell you, that I saw in a dream, they are bringing a very large loom home." She bounced with excitement. "With everything that's been going on, I think I forgot to tell you. I know how to weave. I was taking art classes, in pottery, weaving, and spinning when the war happened. I'm sure I can work that into something useful. If only they could find a pottery wheel and kiln. We could make all kinds of useful things with those."

A noisy hubbub burst into the great room of the cave. Colby riding on his father's back. Ben, Winshaw, Ashling and Jandy danced about the two men, hugging them. All four of the kids speaking at once. "You should see all the cool things they brought." "They have a huge flatbed trailer, heaped with stuff under a tarp." "They have a big mirror." "And a bike for me." Colby yelled above them all.

Their cave was full of laughter, so happy to have the two men home.

# CHAPTER TWENTY-THREE

Nyler watched them work while he held the disconnected power lines, ready to hook them to the solar panels.

"Hand me that wrench," Jack said to Ashling, "And hold the solar plate still, Ben." Then he and Winshaw set the last of seventeen solar panels in place and tightened the bolts to hold them. Until they could go back to Jacks for the array that were still at his place, this was all they could find that looked sound. They had used three generators to make one work. At least for now. They would still have to cook and heat with fire. But at least they would eventually have a steady light to live by when they needed it.

Nyler and Shabda were getting married tomorrow. All was arranged and the people were happy.

That night when they were all gathered around the fire, Jack and Kadora gave Nyler and Shabda a beautiful quilt that Adam and Jack had found out on their hunt. "It's from all of us." Jack said. "You brought us together, Nyler, and we know we are in a better place because of you."

"No. Actually it was the Cats that brought us together." Nyler said holding the beautiful quilt, feeling the softness and the time and love it must have taken to make, thankful for the hands that crafted such comfort and utility. "The Sand Cats, Dream Cats, and the White, all colors, Dragon."

Colby smiled at Nyler. "Did you know that when a Cat loses a whisker it turns into a feather." The boy said. "I have two of them now. A gray feather and a white feather. I think the Cats are actually angels." Then he showed us his two feathers. Nyler and the others were properly impressed. It certainly set Nyler to thinking. Wondering, as it seemed to move them all to consider the true nature of the Cats.

They ate, talked, laughed. Shared their dreams, both their day and night dreams until they all went out to watch the moon rise, big, full and beautiful.

"Look!" Colby whisper in awe, "The Dragon."

To be true... they all saw it fly in front of the brilliant moon, riding the sea breeze.

No one spoke the rest of the evening. The awe was pressed down firmly and blessings were running over the edges of every full heart that night. Enough and to spare.

*****

The men had found an old clawfoot tub and they placed it close to the spring and pool. Made it private with curtains and a fire close by to heat the water. They had all used it since setting it up. But today the ladies were tending to Shabda's bath and the dressing and wedding preparations.

Everyone else was waiting at the caves mouth where the ledge widened enough for all of them to wait for the bride in the coming moonlight.

"Settle down, Nyler," Jack laughed. "Stop pacing or you'll wear a grove across our path."

"They will come when they are ready." Adam sang the words. Grinning. He took a deep breath, "I remember when I was in your shoes, only it was a church floor they told me to stop wearing a hole in. I can't tell you how many times I was told the same thing we're telling you."

"Oh, oh, here they come!" Colby shouted excitedly. "And the moon is almost full up."

It was a warm evening, blessed with a clear, star sparked blue sky, fading to indigo. The moon smiling on them.

Nyler had eyes only for Shabda. She for him. She wore the same white dress as Kadora had worn when she and Jack got married. Nyler stepped forward and took her hand and led her to Jack, who was going to speak the words of bonding, Jack's voice uncertain, for the first time since Nyler had known him.

Jack pulled a scrap of paper from his pocket, and read nervously. "Love is a Song. It sings from each heart standing here before me." He looked into each face shining in the moonlight. "All of you gathered here." He stuffed the bit of paper back in his pocket. "There are so many things we have to do differently these days because the world was broken, the door of war was unhinged, and flung open by lies. We are here because of the truth of love. And now there is a healing happening. There is hope for a better future for all of us."

"Come on, Jack," Colby whispered, "Get to the good stuff." Making every one laugh. Even Jack.

"As you have already expressed your desire to spend your life together, so be it. To each other, to all of us. We acknowledge your commitment and will support you in every way we can. As family, as our Peaceable Community expands." Jack said. "You may kiss your wife. You may kiss your husband. Amen."

And they did. To which Colby said, "Ohhh, yuck." Grimacing "Now can we eat cake?"

The little guy would forever be their comic relief. They did eat cake with a small glass of milk from a goat they found wandering in the neighborhood.

The night was sweet with celebration and thankfulness. Gratitude for the love that made it so.

When Nyler and Shabda retired to their bed niche carved from stone, no one joined them inside the cave. They all slept outside on the entrance ledge, bathed in moonlight.

*****

Nyler was just coming outside the entrance as the sun came up when he saw a new Sand Cat come out of the bushes of the old trail down to Sea Side. Ashling was up so fast and out of her blankets yelling, that it woke everyone else. People rubbing their eyes.

"What's going on?" Jack stood and helped Kadora to her feet.

"What's the matter." Kadora looked around, mystified.

Then Nyler saw the dirty, disheveled young woman coming through the bushes after the Cat. He realized she was pregnant. Then he realized who it was.

"Rita!" Ashling stood in a defensive posture. Hands made into fists. She was looking behind Rita as if she thought Dan might materialize behind the girl. Rita fell to the ground, clutching her stomach, screaming. "Help me!" She gasped, "Please. Help me."

Adam was up and at her side in seconds. The men lifted her onto a blanket and carried her into the cave, where the women and Adam preceded to prepare for the birth of Rita's baby.

Ashling stayed outside watching the bushes by the old overgrown path.

"He's not here. It's alright Ashling." Nyler said. "Jubilee woke me up. That's why I was outside. I wasn't exactly sure who was coming, but I knew it was only one person, and that that person needed our help."

"I don't trust her." Ashling spun around to face him. "She was with him! He's a killer."

"But you know that after he killed those men, she left him. We don't know what her life has been like since."

"Exactly!" Ashling went to the edge of the ledge and looked down the cliff as far as she could see. "Jump showed her coming. That's why I woke up so fast."

"Ash…" Nyler, whispered, "We need to keep an open mind, and heart."

She looked at him with squinted eyes. "You never call me that."

"Ashling, like all of us. She has a story. A life. And a Dream Cat led her here. Don't you think there is room for her too? Room for her baby?"

"Come on Ash," Ben took her hand. "Rita wasn't a bad sort. She was like me and my mom, a captive. She wasn't pregnant by choice. We all had to do things we didn't want to…"

"Let's give her a chance." Winshaw agreed.

"I need Heartsease." Ashling said, looking at Nyler with sad eyes. She turned and hurried toward the west side path to their sacred gathering place of silent listening and reflection.

*****

It was a baby girl, an alarmingly underweight, small infant. But could she cry, until the beautiful dark tabby that had come with Rita, snuggled up next to her and began purring. That tiny scrap of humanity quieted and closed her eyes and slept soundly for a couple of hours.

"Rita has no milk to give. She is far to scrawny herself to be healthy." Adam said. "Are any of the goats we gathered able to give us some milk? I know how to conduct a birthing, not much about feeding a baby under these circumstances."

"We will take care of that!" Maggie said, taking the care of mother and baby in hand. "She needs food herself. Her milk might still come in. I've known of such things happening."

*****

When Ashling came back, she was subdued. She helped Maggie, Kadora, and Shabda with all the extra chores it took to feed an infant. After a week of being quieter than Nyler had ever seen Ashling, he could tell she was falling in love with little baby, Clover. They all were. How could you not. And Rita was up and helping with chores, too. Becoming.

That evening as they all gathered around the firepit after dinner, Rita nursing Clover, as Maggie had hoped would happen, Ashling asked, "What happened to you, Rita? Where did you come from? How did you find us up here?"

Rita looked around the faces turned towards her. "Well... Tiger here," She indicated the great handsome tabby, "He found me in the basement of a burned-out home. I was hiding from Dan. I didn't know then that Dan was gone." Rita gazed at the face of her now sleeping baby. "After... Well, Tiger has shown me things." She paused.

Nyler gave her an encouraging nod of his head. "Go on."

"Everyone I knew was dead, when Danby found me two years ago." Her eyes are huge with memory. "I thought I'd been saved. I had been so afraid... All the time. I kept moving, until I came to Sea Side. I was only fifteen. I spent that first year taking care of the kitchen, with you Maggie... And other girls like me. He collected them. Girls and women. Sometimes they would just disappear. He'd say he sold them, or that they'd run away. Then he made me understand why they would do such a thing."

She looked down at little Clover. "Anyway, when he killed his own watchman that day in your house, I was determined to run away myself. I don't think he even looked for me... even though this is his baby too." She looked so sad then. "He didn't care I was unhappy." She sniffed, and rubbed at her eyes with her free hand. "I have spent these past couple of months trying to keep myself alive and hiding out from everyone, anyone... It was like I had stepped back into my old life again. Then Tiger came to me... Dreamed with me. I had begun to think I would die. Alone and unloved. I didn't know what to do when it was time for the baby to come. Tiger showed me where to find the doctor... To find all of you. A place we could be safe. And since I've been here, I've had a dream that the men who Dan was waiting for never came. Dan left after he saw a giant white dragon flying over the ruins. Anyway, that is what I saw in a dream before Tiger brought me up here. No one is left down there. No one! I think those men all saw a giant white dragon, too, and ran away. We saw it too, Tiger and I. And I wasn't afraid anymore. I just knew if I could make it up here... We'd be alright. We'd be... safe."

* * * * *

Life fell into routines, problems to work out. A jackhammer to repair. Rooms to make. Land to survey. A couple of months into this comfortable pace of life new people began arriving. From as far away as five hundred miles. Two of those people were Jacks two missing brothers.

Michael and Tess and their young son, Jesse. And the youngest brother Larry, and his wife Molly. More people meant more to workout. But the people were accommodating and respectful of each other. Some took up living in the houses that were less damaged but close by and our Peaceable Community grew, people of all colors, many beliefs, many views about how to live life well. Yes, there were dust up now and then disagreements and we'd get everyone together and hear each other out. Talk. Listen. Talk some more. Listen some more, arriving at what we could all live with for the common good, because we agreed love was to be at the center. Truth was to be the guiding principle.

People didn't always change their views, but we learned to respect them as they were. We learned to solve, and resolve problems according to the needs of the people. Love for each other was the understanding. Wanting that common good for all.

People were tired of war and violence. So, we worked at it. Some times that work was harder than other times. But it worked and the hope of the people won the day for another day to come. And the Community grew.

As the years passed, Ashling and Ben married, Jandy and Winshaw married. Surprise of surprises, Adam and Rita married, blessing the community with several more children. Filling our cave and homes with the merry play and laughter of bright children. Many others came, with Cats and dreams that led them here.

Shabda and I had two boys and a girl. How can I express my happiness? The life I had been called to. Jack and Kadora had two girls. Twins.

Our lives progressed and were full of blessings.

In almost what seemed like the blink of an eye. We found our children grown with children of their own.

My life's full joy came with grandchildren, then greatgrandchildren. We, the original ones with our names on the lentil stone, found ourselves in our waning years. The younger generations doing the work, keeping things moving forward. And we thrived.

# CHAPTER TWENTY-FOUR

The Peaceable Community grew, and some went out as I had done and planted other Peaceable Communities to find the lost and alone, to gather them in. To breathe trust back into the human heart and mind.

Hope renewed. A new way of being together. Living as Kin with the earth, each other, and the animals, with the Love that created all this vast world. This universe of truth and beauty. This recognizable gift to us all. We were blessed with long and happy lives in the arms of Mother Terrra.

But no one lives forever and those of us who were now old, began to slip away to the Land Beyond After. Jack and Kadora.

Even Shabda... Nyler ached with the longing he felt to see her, hold her, he knew that everyone in the Community would miss him as they had missed, Jack, Kadora and Shabda.

Shabda, word of truth. His true heart.

How long ago had it been when his Jubilee had shown him Shabda weeping over her Cat.

She had been his word of truth. How he had loved her. Loved her still.

How they loved their children all the way down to the youngest great grands, and great, great grands. Nyler's memories visiting him, so much good, back over his ninety-eight years of life. *So much good.*

Nyler sat out on the ledge overlooking the ocean in a chair he had carved from a teakwood tree, many, many years ago. The sun was going down. The colors spectacular, the clouds in sky becoming like dimpled hammered brass as far as the eye could see. He breathed in the beauty, the song that chorused across the wine dark sea and now changing to vermillion clouds.

Many of the Communities Cats sat with him in the evening as the sun went down, keeping him company. He drifted off to sleep, grateful for all the years of his life.

*****

He and Jubilee slipped into a dream.

They were walking up a grassy green hill. Light streaming from everything, everywhere he looked was beauty that pierced his heart with such gladness. He could hear singing... and laughter. Then he saw Shabda, and his mother and father. His brother who died when they were boys. Jack and Kadora. A crowd of people he recognized coming to greet him, some of whom he had never met, but had seen in Jubilee's dreams. Zada Zan, her mother, Avril with all of their people behind them.

His heart was full and over flowing.

The Sea of Time. Ships on the Sea of Time.

It was his point of transfer. His people... Love was coming to welcome him home. He and Jubilee were going to a new Peaceable Community.

Made in the USA
Columbia, SC
12 October 2024

43521530R00072